ALBANY HOUSE
PART TWO
THE
HOMECOMING

Nigel Heath

This is a work of fiction. Names, characters, business, events and incidents are the products of the author's imagination. Any resemblance to actual persons, living or dead, or actual events is purely coincidental.

Copyright © Nigel Heath 2022
This book is sold subject to the condition that it shall not, by way of trade or otherwise, be lent, resold, hired out, or otherwise circulated without the publisher's prior consent in any form of binding or cover other than that in which it is published and without a similar condition including this condition being imposed on the subsequent publisher.
The moral right of Nigel Heath has been asserted.

ISBN: 9798362019075

My grateful thanks in the preparation of Albany House are due to Marc Bessant Design, my wife, Jenny Davis, Mary Watts and Alexandra Bridger for literary support, to artist Maureen Langford for the cover picture and to my walking companion and poet, Peter Gibbs, for his technical support. Peter's poetry anthology, Let The Good Rhymes Roll, is also published on Amazon.

Chapter 1

Miss Charlotte Andrews had reached her seventieth year and was still as fit as fiddle and as bright as a button and always insisted on taking a long afternoon constitutional along the Sidmouth prom and onto the steeply rising coastal path beyond, as long as there was a willing arm on which to hold.

She didn't actually need the arm, but enjoyed the brief human contact. There was never normally any shortage of arms because it was a chance to escape and she was always a pleasure to be with and, as this was a seriously upmarket and exclusive retirement hotel set in extensive grounds overlooking the sea, the residents' wishes were the management's commands.

All the 'guests' at Ocean View, this former Victorian hotel, were free to come and go as they pleased, which did pose a small problem in Miss Charlotte's case, because when she went off on one of her 'jaunts,' no one was quite sure when she might return, although it was usually within twenty-four hours. Not for the first time they'd received a call on her mobile, requesting a car to come and pick her up from further along the coast at Seaton or Lyme Regis, or some other place, where she'd suddenly gone on a whim and knowing full well that it was unlikely there would be a bus back.

While she was known to all as 'Miss Charlotte,' she was actually Mrs Charlotte Andrews, whose stepson, James, a wealthy property developer based in the Caribbean, had made it clear that he had a bottomless pocket as far as the requirements and comforts of his 'Ma' were concerned.

He'd advised them, when she took up residence, of her tendency to go walk about and was paying an additional premium for the hotel team to take special care of her, because she had no relatives in the UK and he was over 4,000 miles away.

Guests were required to sign in and out so that the management had some idea of how many could be expected for lunch or dinner in the spacious silver service dining room overlooking the hotel's extensive flower-filled gardens. True to her nature, Miss Charlotte hardly ever bothered to sign the book, regarding it as something of an imposition, but as she was the only one to ignore this house rule, it did not much matter from a catering perspective, but it did make it more difficult to keep tabs on her. When she was in residence, she could always be found sitting in her favourite armchair by the big picture window in the comfortable lounge, but if it was found to be empty, then the discreet call would go out: "Has anyone seen Miss Charlotte?"

This particular sunny June afternoon, it was answered by Annie Willmott, Ocean View's Senior Duty Manger, who was particularly fond of their spirited and independently-minded guest. She'd last 'found' Miss Charlotte in a small pagoda-style summerhouse at the top of the grounds, hidden by a late- flowering clump of rhododendrons and with a bird's eye view over the town, and made her way straight to it,

"There you are Miss Charlotte. Are you enjoying the view?" There was a faraway look in her eyes. "I think it's time I went home," she replied softly. "But your stepson lives in the Caribbean, so is that where you want to go?" Annie asked.

"No, I don't want to return to the Caribbean, I want to go back to my real home where I grew up and was the happiest."

Annie was a little surprised. She'd spent many hours in Miss Charlotte's company, but never had she mentioned where she'd come from. "And where is home, Miss Charlotte?" she asked. quietly. "It's a small place in North Devon called Little Oreford." Annie sat down on the seat beside her.

"I'd just like to see the old place one last time. I left when I was a young woman and never went back, which was a great sadness in my life." She sighed. "Would you like to talk about that?" "No, dear, I'd rather not." There was a wistful expression on the old woman's face as she turned and looked up at Annie.

"But would you take me back there, dear, in your little red car and perhaps we might stay somewhere thereabouts just for a couple of days?" Annie said that would be nice, but she was not sure if she would be allowed to.

"And why not? It can be charged to my account. It's high time I had a holiday and it will be a sort of thank you for all your little kindnesses to me." Annie had got to know Ocean View's VIP guest during their regular strolls along the esplanade and it had become clear quite early on that underneath a kindly exterior, she was strong-willed and liked having her own way.

Most of the retirement hotel's other guests were self-assured ex- professional people, but all had learned not to sit in Miss Charlotte's favourite armchair. Annie was not at all sure just how much of a holiday it would be looking after this elderly guest with a mind of her own once they were out on the loose together. Still the idea did have some appeal. She was between boyfriends and

had, although she'd not admit it, started feeling the odd pang of loneliness. "The Directors would have to see what your stepson thought," she said tentatively.
"Oh, James won't give a fig, so that's settled then," said Miss Charlotte, a smile lighting up her still mostly amazingly clear- skinned face, "I'm not sure it is quite settled yet," Annie countered as they got up to leave the summerhouse. But surprisingly it was settled because James Andrews, the hugely wealthy boss of World-Wide Island Homes in the Sun, hadn't the slightest objection to his stepma having a little holiday accompanied by Ocean View's Senior Duty Manager.

Hotel Joint Directors and proprietors Sam and Sally Owen were only too happy to accede to the wishes of their wealthiest client, who paid their most expensive rate to ensure the old lady was well looked after. That evening when Annie got back to her flat in one of the seaside town's large former Victorian family residences that had mostly all seen sunnier days, she got out her laptop and Googled 'Places to stay in Little Oreford' and up popped The Oreford Inn, a 16th century coaching inn with four en-suite rooms so that might work, she thought. Two afternoons later, her bosses called her in for a pre-holiday briefing, where she learned that instructions had come from the Caribbean that no expense was to be spared in granting Miss Charlotte her holiday wish. These were the sort of instructions the Owens particularly liked to receive, because it meant they could charge Annie out at a full and inflated rate and if the few days should happen to turn into a week or two then more was the better, as Sam had put it to his wife. "We're not quite sure your estate car would really be suitable for this expedition, so we're hiring a chauffeur-driven Bentley, which will relieve you of the responsibility and allow you to devote your full attention to Miss Charlotte," he announced.

Annie opened her mouth to suggest there was really no need to go to all that trouble, but quickly shut it again when her boss pointed out that this was the best solution from Ocean View's insurance perspective. "Perish the thought that you might just be involved in some road accident, clearly at no fault of your own, with one of our guests in your car," he pointed out.

"So, getting down to the planning, have you made any progress in researching where you might stay in Little Oreford and when you might go, Annie?" his wife, Sally, asked. She told them about the Oreford Inn that offered luxury B&B and full board rates and had vacancies for the beginning of the third week in July.

"Miss Charlotte says that now she's made up her mind to go on holiday, it can be the sooner the better, so I guess we'll aim to go then if that's OK with you."

Now that all had been settled, and although just a little apprehensive at the prospect of playing companion, Annie began looking forward to her out of the blue holiday. Her life had slipped into a rut after her boyfriend of four years had suddenly up and ditched her for another. Losing Matt had really sent her under and for months it was as much as she could do to keep on turning up for work, but the shadows over her life had begun melting away of late and now there was to be this complete break from her routine and best of all it wasn't going to cost her a bean!

Chapter 2

"Isn't this exciting, Annie. We're on our way at last," said Miss Charlotte, taking hold of her young companion's arm as the black limousine pulled smoothly away from Ocean View. The Owens had come out to see her off, while Bill, their resident gardener and handyman, had helped Bob the chauffeur load the luggage.

"We're just going to have such fun and it's going to be a real adventure, so I can't think why I didn't have this idea years ago. Maybe if all goes well, we might have another little jaunt later in the year." Annie said that would be lovely, although she wasn't sure she meant it.

"Everything OK in the back, ladies. Let me know if you want some air con, because I think the day's going to be a hot one," said Bob through his intercom.

"He seems a very nice young man," said Miss Charlotte. Annie smiled to herself because Bob was probably in his early forties. So, if Bob was young, then she must be a mere child, although at the age of thirty-two she wasn't quite ready to be joining the 'ladies.'

Miss Charlotte asked how long the journey was going to take and Bob told her that, according to his Sat Nav, it would be three hours and fifteen minutes via the M5.

"Oh! do we have to go on the motorway? It's a lovely day

and just finding our way along country roads with all their lovely green hedges and trees would be so much nicer, especially as we have a picnic, don't you think, Bob?".
"We can do, but it would make the journey quite a bit longer. What do you think, Miss Willmott?" he asked.
"Well, it's Miss Charlotte's holiday, so I guess it's really up to her."
Bob switched the Sat Nav to non-motorway mode and told them their arrival time had now moved back from 2pm to 3.45pm.
They'd been making their way West to pick up the M5 at Exeter, but now the route was weaving its way more or less straight across country. Still, it was no odds to him. He was with them all week and he didn't really mind where they went.
Bob Smart was a bit of a loner. He'd never married and had lived with his mum until her death some years earlier. He'd always been a driver in one form or another, but was never a trucker because that seemed to him to be rather an uncomfortable occupation and didn't match with his more refined sensibilities and his preference for being at home and listening to his music most evenings. He'd found his ideal role some years earlier working for a local funeral director, because that meant always wearing a smart dark suit and keeping his motors

gleaming. Then when his mother died, he'd sold their seafront semi for a considerable sum, bought a ground floor apartment in a spacious new block and invested a considerable portion of the residue in his own classic Bentley. It had been superbly maintained and was his personal pride and joy.

Bob discovered, somewhat to his surprise, that when it came to private enterprise, he was definitely no slouch, and had built up a nice little business being available for weddings and funerals, which were his bread and butter, and also for private hire.

Like Annie, he was viewing this commission as a bit of a surprise holiday and had found himself a B&B close to Little Oreford in a village called Hampton Green.

It was a converted barn run by two ladies and almost next door to the pub where he was assured the food was exceptionally good.

."Maybe you could look out for a nice spot where we could have our lunch, Bob," Miss Charlotte suggested as it was approaching noon." "What do you think Annie?" She wasn't really hungry but as luncheon at Ocean View was always served promptly at 12.30pm, she guessed her companion was ready to eat. "That's fine by me, Miss Charlotte."

Shortly afterwards, spotting a small lake surrounded by picnic benches with tables and accessed by a car park, he pulled in. There were a couple of youngsters fishing and a family having a picnic. "It's just perfect," announced Miss Charlotte, gazing out over the lake after she and Annie had settled themselves at one of the tables. She'd invited Bob to join them and help himself to one of the smoked salmon and cream cheese sandwiches, but he'd declined saying he'd stretch his legs with a walk around the lake. After all they were his clients and it was a question of respect. "He seems a very nice young man, but perhaps a bit lonely," she remarked once he was out of earshot. "How can you tell, Miss Charlotte, because we don't know anything about him?" She smiled. "I just have that feeling, dear." Oh, no, it was the second time she'd said how nice Bob was, so she hoped this wasn't a match-making attempt just to complicate things. They watched Bob's solitary progress as they ate and until they were disturbed by a middle-aged couple passing by with a frisky young Labrador. Miss Charlotte immediately engaged them in conversation because Labs, she told them, were her favourites.

This was not true because she'd absolutely no interest in dogs whatsoever, but she did like chatting to people and that's how she found things out. Their chauffeur returned just as the couple had said their goodbyes.

"Oh, Bob, I thought it a little strange there are so few people here on such a lovely day, but that's because it's the village fete this afternoon and that's where everyone is, so do we have time to pop in, just for ten minutes or so?" He looked at Annie for guidance but she didn't have the heart to dampen her spirits, although she did have a sort of helpless feeling that she and Bob were already losing their grip on the situation. The look on his face suggested he felt the same way too, but what could they do?

The Chairman of the Swanley Fete Committee had broken out in a cold sweat. It was now gone 2pm and their opener, a minor TV soap star, who just happened to live in the neighbourhood, had not turned up and was not answering her mobile. The special little podium from which she was to make her speech was all set up with its attending microphone and the fete, set amid trees festooned with bunting, was now in full swing. "If she's much later, we'll have to stop the proceedings for her to open them again," the chairman muttered to his equally anxious wife, waiting nervously at his side, as he glanced at his watch for the umpteenth time.

The couple were standing out in the lane and greeting the trickle of villagers still making their way to the fete. "Try calling her again, dear?" his wife suggested, but just as she did so they both spotted the chauffeur-driven car coming slowly towards them.

"Thank God for that," muttered the chairman, who wouldn't have known their minor celebrity from Eve, as he and his wife made a point of never watching soaps.

A parking space just inside the orchard had been reserved for their special guest, so he stepped out into the road and waved the Bentley through the gate. There were two women sitting in the back and he assumed the older one, who'd just given him a regal wave, was their soap star. 'She's a bit elderly, so maybe she plays a grandmother or something,' he thought.

Bob and Annie were puzzled. Something wasn't quite right here, but Miss Charlotte was delighted. "What lovely considerate people, Annie, to show us in like this." Just then, the chairman's phone burst into life in his top pocket. His first instinct was to ignore it as their emergency was now over, but like many, he was a slave to it and couldn't resist tearing it from his pocket and answering it, pressing the loudspeaker button in his haste.

"Is that someone at the Swanley fete?" It was a woman's voice and she did not sound well and if the chairman had not known any better, then he'd have said she was the worst for drink. "I'm most terribly sorry. I've gone down with a ghastly runny tummy, which came on just as I was about to drive over to you." The absent star had, in fact, been on a bender with friends the night before and had not long regained her wits, groggy as they still were. Bob had climbed out of the Bentley and was already opening the door for Miss Charlotte and Annie, as the chairman's wife approached. It seemed clear to her that this extremely well-dressed and most refined looking elderly lady was indeed their VIP.

"We're awfully glad you've come," she said stepping forward to shake her hand. "I'm really happy to be here, dear." Bob and Annie glanced at one another as the penny collectively dropped. These people thought Miss Charlotte was some special guest! Now the chairman was at his wife's side, hurriedly explaining the misunderstanding and saying how they could keep the parking space because their VIP opener wasn't coming after all.

"Don't worry I'd be happy to open your lovely fete for you," offered Miss Charlotte, looking around and seeing that the Bentley's arrival had already drawn a small

crowd and that she was now the centre of attention. Bob and Annie just looked at one another in astonishment.
"That's awfully kind of you," said the chairman, seeing a way out of this embarrassing situation suddenly opening up in front of him. Stepping forward, he took Miss Charlotte's arm and gently escorting her towards the podium, was thinking wildly about just how he was going to introduce her. "You can say that your opener has been taken ill and that I, Lady Charlotte Andrews, have graciously volunteered to take her place," she suggested, as if she had just been reading her thoughts. Walking just a couple of paces behind, Bob and Annie exchanged hurried glances. Could this really be happening?

The chairman did as he was instructed. Miss Charlotte, completely unphased, waited as the microphone was lowered to her level, and then addressing the crowd, said she was delighted to be attending their fete on such a glorious afternoon and hoped they'd all have a lovely time.

There followed a ripple of applause from all the villagers standing around the scattering of gaily decorated stalls and Charlotte turned around to take the chairman's arm.

"Would you like my wife and I to escort you around our stalls Lady Charlotte?" he asked still not quite believing all that had just happened. "I'd be delighted, my dear." Annie stole a glance at her watch. At this rate who knows what time they'd get to Little Oreford, but luckily after a quarter of an hour, she was ready to leave, but definitely now on a 'high.

"Just think, if we hadn't chatted to that nice couple by the lake, we'd never have known about the fete, but I hope it hasn't delayed us too much, Bob?" she said. " Don't worry Miss Charlotte because we'll still be there at a reasonable time," he assured her. "Oh, dear, Bob. Can we now stop all this 'Miss Charlotte' business because it makes me feel in some way superior, which of course I'm not, so for the rest of the holiday you can both call me Charlie. That's what my friends all called me when I was young." Annie was on the point of asking about her growing up in Little Oreford, but then remembered their conversation in the summerhouse where she'd gained the distinct impression that she'd been reluctant to talk about her childhood.

Chapter 3

It was around 6pm when the holiday party finally rolled into Little Oreford, cruised past the picture postcard village green and drew up outside the inn. "Wait here, ladies. I'll just nip in and see where I'm to park." But before he could leave the car, a young man who'd been watering hanging baskets packed with bright red geraniums, put down his can and directed them towards a parking area just at the end of the green. While Bob was unloading the cases, Annie suggested Charlie might like to stay by the car for a few moments while she went to check in.

The old stone pillared gate at the end of the car park clearly led into some large mansion, Bob noted while walking around to the boot, but the effect on Charlie was overwhelming. Here they were outside dear old Albany House, the former Little Oreford rectory, and her childhood home. Now she was a girl again and playing hopscotch in the road beside the green on chalked squares with her best friends, Robin and Margo, who lived in that cottage over there. She turned her gaze away from the gates to where she knew their cottage would surely be.

Then her thoughts turned to later and much darker times and to that autumn afternoon she'd flounced out of the house having rowed bitterly with her parents, the Rev and Mrs Will Potter and vowing never to return. She was three months pregnant out of wedlock as a result of one unplanned encounter and had brought utter disgrace on her oh so bloody holier than thou family. She could still see the anger in her father's eyes, her mother looking on with cold indifference and the undisguised smirk on the face of her older sister, Cynthia, who'd always despised her for being everything she herself was not. She'd kept her promise and never returned, but now after all these years, she knew in her heart she was pleased to have come back, if only for a few precious days.

Lost in thought, she stepped away from the car and was now standing just inside the entrance gates and gazing at the Victorian rectory. Like her playmates' cottage, little seemed to have changed, but she wasn't sure the house had an entrance porch when she was a girl.

Bob had also been lost in his own thoughts as he was lifting the two cases out of the boot, because he was suddenly finding himself strongly attracted to Annie, whose shapely figure he'd followed appreciatively as she walked towards the inn. 'Time for a reality check, Robert. This is highly unprofessional and besides that, what's she going to see in you so dream on sunshine,' he told himself, closing the boot with far more force than usual as if to close down the daydream.

"Bob. Where's Miss Charlotte?" There was alarm in Annie's voice and he looked hurriedly around. "She was standing right there by the car just a moment ago," he explained. "Well, she's not there now." There was a small and hurtful accusation in her tone. They both scanned the empty green and then Bob's gaze returned to the stone gate posts just a few paces from the car. "She's got to have gone in there," he muttered, moving swiftly towards the leafy entrance. "Miss Charlotte," called Annie now following their chauffeur into the tree-lined drive, where they both spotted their charge standing on the edge of a highly manicured lawn and gazing towards a large Victorian house.

"There you are Miss Charlotte, I mean Charlie," said Annie in a voice that announced relief. "Yes. Here I am dear. Is anything the matter?" Her hearing was still remarkably sharp and her intellect had already told her that she'd alarmed them, and in that moment, she felt a sense of annoyance.

She'd been around for more years than Annie and Bob put together and she resented being treated like some naughty child. It was shades of her childhood coming back to haunt her. 'If I'm to have a holiday I want to be free to wander about as I like and not to be minded over every moment of the day and night,' she told herself. Annie was a lovely girl and Bob seemed a nice young man but she'd have to make them understand that they were not to behave like her minders.

Goodness it was like having her parents getting cross with her when she was late home for tea or had refused to wear that ridiculous pink frilly dress for her father's annual Rector's tea party on the lawn behind the house.

"Are we all booked in then, dear?" she asked, swiftly returning herself to the present. "Yes. All done, Miss Charlotte, I mean Charlie," she said, having so quickly forgotten her wishes for a second time in all the panic. "They've given us two adjoining rooms overlooking the green and the nice woman on reception has reserved a table in the restaurant for 7.30pm, if that's OK," said Annie moving forward and taking Charlie's arm as she had done so many times before on their afternoon strolls along the prom back at home.

The coaching inn's big main bar had already started filling up with locals supping an early evening pint and a younger set enjoying pre-dinner drinks. Reception was in a recess in the large flag-stoned hall leading towards the toilets and a stable yard, where several families were occupying wooden tables with benches. The manageress, a pretty woman in her early forties, made a special point of welcoming Charlie and hoping she would enjoy her stay with them as she handed over their room keys to Annie. But Charlie wasn't listening. She was staring intently at the smart name badge which read 'Corinne Potter, Manager.'

She'd never told Annie, or anyone else at Ocean View, about her past or that she'd once been Little Oreford rector's daughter, Miss Charlotte Potter, a lifetime before she'd married wealthy property developer Hugo Andrews. It was all too complicated and besides she'd spent most of her life pushing uncomfortable memories to the back of her mind. But now standing behind the hotel reception was a young woman with the same name as the daughter, who'd been removed from her a life time ago.

There was something undeniably familiar about the young woman, but how could it possibly be that the baby she'd so reluctantly given up for adoption at six months old had somehow found her way to back to Little Oreford?

Suddenly it was all too much. "I'm feeling a little faint, so do you think we might sit down for a moment?" she asked, turning to Annie. Corinne Potter came out from behind the reception desk and guided them both to a leather sofa and hurried off for a glass of water. "It must be the long journey and all the excitement of opening the fete and everything," Annie suggested, but Charlie didn't hear her, so lost was she in a whole maze of thoughts and feelings.

She'd so wanted to come back to Little Oreford to wander around, just remembering her childhood and all the happy times she'd spent with Robin and Margo, and perhaps finally coming to terms with all the unhappiness that followed. But to suddenly be confronted by her daughter, because Charlie had absolutely no doubt that Corinne Potter was her daughter, was simply all too much.

Corinne returned with the glass of water and caught a sad almost beseeching look in her elderly guest's still bright blue eyes as she handed it to her. "Are you all right?" she asked in a voice full of concern. There was a warmth in that voice and it somehow comforted Charlie. "Yes. I'll be all right in a minute," she replied, beginning to pull herself together.

Their adjoining rooms were large and comfortable and Charlie's had an easy chair by the window looking out onto the green. "Would you like me to help you unpack before we go down to dinner?" Annie suggested.

"No, dear, I'm quite happy to do that myself but I don't think I'll come down again tonight. It's been quite a long and exciting day, what with opening that fete and everything.

"So, I'll just stay here and sit awhile in that chair overlooking the green and perhaps they could bring me up some assorted sandwiches." Annie was not at all displeased at the prospect of enjoying a quiet meal in her own company.

Gazing out over the green, Charlie began coming to terms with the incredible realisation that her daughter was downstairs. But just how on earth could that possibly be, she wondered. Yet simply knowing she'd grown up, looked well and had found a place in life was a blessing. So maybe that was enough and there was no need to reveal she was the mother who'd abandoned her.

'Don't be so stupid. How could you possibly just walk away without telling her and finding out how she'd, completely unknowingly, found her way back to Little Oreford?' she immediately challenged herself. But then another uncomfortable reality pressed in on her as she thought of Corinne's twin sister Laura.

Oh! how she'd agonised in despair gazing down at one tiny child and then the other, trying to decide which precious baby to give away and which one to try and keep. Harsh reality had told her that with no means of supporting either twin, she should let them both go, but that she could not bear to do.

Charlie's eyes filled with tears as she again struggled to come to terms with the unspoken anguish which had returned to haunt her again and again throughout her life, but had eventually mercifully faded into the shadows until now.

Finding Corinne and being so forcefully confronted by her past. was more than a shock. Yet, essentially, Charlie was, and always had been, a strong person with an optimistic nature, which had eventually seen her safely through her troubled years. She should rejoice over finding Corinne again and trust that somewhere in the world, all would be well with Laura, she told herself. Charlie made up her mind to concentrate on that positive thought, rather than allowing all the past anguish to seep back into her heart.

Now her eye came to rest on the attractive white-washed thatched cottage immediately opposite, which had been Robin and Margo's home. 'I'll try my best to think about them for now,' Charlie told herself as firmly as she could. Her friend's real name was Margaret, but she'd decided one day that she'd prefer to be called Margo. "If you're going to be Margo, then I'm going to be Charlie, because I absolutely hate Charlotte," she'd announced.

Smiling to herself, she recalled the almighty row there'd been when she returned to the rectory and told her parents of her intention. The Rev Potter said he 'wasn't having it' and her mother had agreed, but Charlie, was 'having it' and was very stubborn and not at all like her more compliant sister.

"Honestly, I sometimes wonder where that child has come from," Will Potter complained to his wife after one particularly heated exchange with their wayward daughter. She wasn't meant to have heard the throw-away remark but she'd developed the habit of hovering out of sight and making it her business to hear what her parents were saying about her after she'd flounced out of an argument and had invariably been sent to her room.

Chapter 4

Bob Smart was also deep in thought as he drove slowly down through the narrow lanes towards Hampton Green and his B&B. The sexy image of Annie as she'd walked towards the inn was still exciting him and he thought just how nice it would be to have a woman friend after all these years. His mother had always encouraged the few young women he had brought home, but when they started becoming serious, he'd always backed off and then regretted it afterwards, but now, just maybe, he was ready to allow someone into his life.

He and his mum had lived quietly and happily together after the sudden death of his father, who was essentially a good man, but was opinionated and more than a little domineering. Bob had considered Internet dating but somehow that wasn't for him, or so he kept telling himself, although in his heart of hearts he knew that was a bit of a cop out.

Soon he was driving into Hampton Green and passed The Red Lion, as instructed in his telephone conversation with the lady at the B&B, and taking the drive beside the church to arrive at a large barn conversion. It turned out he had two hosts, who introduced themselves as Heather and Hannah and promptly invited him to join them for an aperitif, after he'd made himself comfortable because, it was too late for a cuppa. All he really wanted to do was to escape to the pub for a quiet pint and a bite to eat, but as he would be staying with them all week, it would have been rather impolite to decline.

Heather, whom he judged to be in her early forties and was slim with short cropped blonde hair, met him at the bottom of the stairs and ushered him into their spacious living-room complete with exposed oak beams, and asked him what he'd like to drink. "I'm easy. I'll have whatever you're having." he said. "Great, so we'll open a bottle of sparkling then shall we, Heather?" said a voice from the kitchen, followed shortly afterwards by the distinctive sound of a cork popping.

Heather invited him to sit on a large cream-coloured leather sofa and sat herself in one of the two arm chairs opposite. "We have a confession to make, haven't we, Han," she said as the other woman entered with three champagne glasses on a silver tray and placed one on a small oak coffee table in front of him. "You have?" said Bob, smiling at Hannah, who was as dark as Heather was fair with a more rounded face and shoulder-length curly hair. He could hardly believe he'd ended up about to drink bubbly with two very attractive women and wondering what on earth was coming next.

"Yes," said Heather. "You are our first ever guest and as you are going to be staying with us for a week, we should be grateful for any tips on how we might improve our service." For a split second, Bob imagined himself in an enormous bed with these two, eager to please, ladies. "Of course, I'd be delighted to, but somehow I don't think that is going to be necessary," he replied.

"The pub gets quite busy on Saturday nights, so we've reserved you a table for 8pm so I hope that's all right," said Hannah, taking the other armchair. "So, what brings you and your superb car to Hampton Green, a wedding perhaps?" she asked.

He told how he'd chauffeured Miss Charlotte and Annie from the Ocean View retirement hotel in Sidmouth to spend a few days at The Oreford Inn in Little Oreford, because the old lady had grown up in the village, and how she'd come to open a fete on the way. "She sounds a real character doesn't she, Heather?" Bob nodded. "She's that all right," he agreed, taking this to be an appropriate moment to get slowly to his feet and escape to the pub for his supper.

While Bob was enjoying his not so quiet pint because the pub was busy, and looking forward to his lamb shank, Annie had finished her supper and had gone upstairs to find Charlie still sitting in her chair with a plate of half-eaten sandwiches by her side and her small suitcase still unopened on the bed. She'd spent most of her time just gazing out over that oh-so-familiar green still coming to terms with the astonishing fact that her own daughter was on the floor below them.

" Can I help you unpack now, Charlie?" she asked, "No, dear, I can manage, but I do have a question to ask. Have you by any chance happened to mention to anyone down stairs that I grew up here?" Annie thought about the unexpected question for a few moments. "No, because we only arrived here a few hours ago and I certainly don't think I mentioned it when I made the booking," she explained. "Does Bob know?" The look on her elderly friend's face was intent. "Yes. I'm sure I've mentioned it to him," she admitted. "Now I want you to promise me that neither of you will mention my having grown up here to anyone." Annie said that, of course, she wouldn't and she'd mention it to Bob when he called. "Good, but there's another thing." Now Annie was wondering just what would be coming next. "You don't need to spend your whole time here looking after me you know. "I shall be quite content wandering around the village tomorrow and probably the next day, so maybe you and Bob might like to take the car and have a little tour around by yourselves." There was a twinkle in her eyes as she spoke and Annie realised full well what was in her mind.

Back in her room, Annie thought about Miss Charlotte's requests to keep the reason for their visit a secret, which was a bit puzzling, and how she wanted to be left on her own to wander about while she and Bob went off for the day. She couldn't just do it without telling her bosses because what on earth would they say if something happened while they were off enjoying the themselves? She switched on the TV and half watched a movie while she thought about the rest of the week and the prospect of spending it with Bob. He seemed a nice enough chap, but if there was going to be nothing for him to do for a couple of days, then perhaps he'd prefer to go home. She supposed there might be a bus she could take into Draymarket, which she'd spotted was the nearest market town, so maybe she should call Bob now in case he'd prefer to make an early start on his drive back. The chauffeur was just leaving the pub when his mobile rang, which was just as well because a few moments earlier he would never have heard it.

No, he told her, going home was not an option, because he'd been booked for a week, as was his B&B, so yes, he'd be delighted to take up Miss Charlotte's kind offer that they should take a little tour together later in the week if that was convenient. So, he would turn up around noon tomorrow, unless she called to say he should come earlier. "One other thing, Bob. For some reason she doesn't want anyone knowing she grew up here so we're both sworn to secrecy."

Now he was in a real spot because he'd already told his hosts the reason for their visit, but should he admit that to Annie? He decided not to because the chances of them telling the people at the pub were pretty minimal. Bob strolled back to the B&B with a growing sense of expectation, finding it difficult to believe that fortune had conspired to smile on him in such an unexpected way, but then it occurred to him that he had absolutely nothing to wear except his chauffeur's uniform and some comfortable well-worn clothes for lazing about in and going out to the pub to eat.

Both Hannah and Heather were about when he let himself in and promptly invited him to join them for a coffee, or something stronger if he preferred, unless, of course, he just wanted to chill out in his room. How could he possibly decline such an invitation from two very attractive woman, he was tempted to say, but instead, he nodded politely, saying that would be nice and that a black coffee with a small brandy, if they had one, would be fine. Again, settled in their spacious lounge, the two began gently quizzing him about his life in general and before he knew it, he was telling them about the small issue of his needing to buy some casual clothes for his little tour around with Annie.

He suddenly felt embarrassed as he sensed them looking him up and down. "What you're wearing is OK," lied Hannah, taking in the heavily-scuffed brown leather shoes, blue jeans that had faded in places through just too many cycles in the washing machine and his red and white checked open-necked shirt that had definitely seen better days. "But perhaps a few new things wouldn't go amiss in these unusual circumstances," she suggested. The truth was that once Bob was out of his impeccably-smart uniform, he just liked to lounge around in old and comfortable things. He did have smarter stuff in his wardrobe, but he hadn't dated anyone for a long time and apart from a stroll down to his local a couple of evenings a week, there wasn't really anything or anybody to dress up for.

"OK. Help is at hand," said Hannah. "I have to drive into Draymarket tomorrow morning to do a shop and to pop into the office. You could come with me and while I'm there you could call in at Milton's, because, believe it or not, the town still has a gent's outfitters. It's been going for years but was taken over recently by young Dan Milton, after his father's retirement and has now gone really quite up market and trendy."

Bob wasn't sure that upmarket and trendy was quiet his style, but still it was worth a go. He could easily drive himself into town and maybe that would be best if he wanted to make sure he was in Little Oreford by noon, but when Hannah assured him, they'd be back in plenty of time, he decided to go with the flow.

He'd assumed his hosts didn't work so wondered what her reference to 'the office' meant, but decided not to pursue it as he was tired and needed to go to bed.

Annie was now in a dilemma. Miss Charlotte had made her wishes quite clear and she knew she would not take too kindly to having a minder trailing around after her. But she couldn't just go swanning off with Bob leaving her to her own devices because, on recent past performance, who knows what she might get up to. Yes, seeking guidance from her employers was her only option, she decided.

Breakfast was from 7.15 am, which suited Annie because she'd always been an early riser, so she got up and went for a stroll around the deserted green before entering the still empty restaurant, where Corinne Potter was bringing out a large bowl of fresh fruit from the kitchen. Spotting a table set for two in the window, she sat down and casually picked up the menu. It seemed surprising that the manager, who'd checked them in, was also on breakfast duty and casually remarked on this when Corinne came over to take her order.

"Oh! it's all hands to the pump around here. Our breakfast girl's not feeling well this morning, so I'm standing in. Did you have a comfortable night?" she asked. "Good thanks and thank you again for the sandwiches you sent up for Miss Charlotte." Corinne said they could also provide a breakfast tray if Miss Charlotte would like one. "That's very kind of you. I'll ask her, although I think she might prefer to come down, but talking of Miss Charlotte, I have something of a favour to ask."

Annie explained her dilemma and wondered if it might be possible for Corinne and her team to keep an eye on their older guest, who'd expressed a wish to be left on her own while she just wandered about the village. "I'm sure we can do that because we're rather like one big family around here.

"My twin sister, Laura, and her husband, Ben, live in the big house next door and my nephew, Luke, helps out here when he's home from university, which he is at the moment. His sister, Lottie, still lives at home and often does waitressing for us if we're a bit pushed, so I'm sure we can all help to keep an eye open for Miss Charlotte."

Finishing her breakfast, Annie went back upstairs to find Charlie awake and sitting up in bed reading one of the complimentary glossy magazines featuring North Devon, which had been displayed on a side table. Yes, a breakfast tray with perhaps a small portion of scrambled eggs would be fine and then perhaps they could go for a stroll around the village around 11am.

When Annie got back to her room, she called Bob, saying there was now no need for him to arrive until after lunch and then spoke to the Owens, telling them of Charlie's request to be left on her own. Sally Owen wasn't sure it was a good idea to allow their most important paying guest to go walkabout, even though the Oreford Inn's staff would be keeping an eye open for her. "I think we'll have to check it out with her stepson first, so see if you can stay with her until we've clarified the situation." Annie said she'd do her best before receiving some further instructions.

But now she began wondering if Miss Charlotte had forgotten all about wanting to be left on her own, seeing they were to go out for a stroll later. She surprised herself by suddenly experiencing a tinge of disappointment at maybe not now being allowed to 'escape' with Bob. How perverse was human nature? When Miss Charlotte suggested the idea, she was not at all sure she wanted to spend a day with rather dull Bob, which had been her initial impression of him, but now it was beginning to look as if it wasn't going to happen, she was rather hoping that it might.

Chapter 5

Breakfast was a slightly embarrassing affair for Bob with both Hannah and Heather fussing over him like two mother hens. As he was their first guest and the ice had certainly been broken after their nightcap the previous evening, they were acting more as if he was some long-lost brother. They'd already discovered he was a fan of quiz nights because there was a weekly one back home at his local, so they'd invited him to join him for theirs at the pub the following evening. "Quiz nights at The Lion are great fun, but underneath it, all the regular teams are highly competitive, so you'll really enjoy it, won't he, Han."

Driving into Draymarket in Hannah's estate car proved to be a slightly uncomfortable experience because he was not accustomed to being a passenger and certainly not to being driven by a woman at a speed well beyond his comfort zone. Roles had been reversed, he was not in control and certainly too embarrassed to ask her if she'd mind slowing down just a little, but a glance across at him told her he was not at his ease and she instantly reduced speed.

"I've driven these lanes so often I guess I do go faster than is probably a good idea," she admitted. She told him how she and Heather had both worked in a London library before coming across Hampton Green on a touring holiday. "The barn was to rent and Royston Randall, the local estate agent, was looking for an assistant, but gave us both a job and the rest as they say is history." "Are you still working there?" he asked. "Yes, but I'm part-time in our village office now, while Heather's very much more involved and runs our head office here in Draymarket," she said as they pulled into High Street. "Head office, sounds like it's quite a big operation," said Bob. "Certainly is. We were just based in Hampton when we joined Royston, but we later took over a rival agency here some years ago and have steadily expanded ever since, so we now pretty much cover the whole of North Devon and a lot of Cornwall. Come to think of it, you must meet Royston, because he's well into his old cars and owns several of them." Pulling off the main road into a narrow side street, they squeezed past a number of parked cars, and into a spacious private parking area where an impeccably-suited Royston Randall was just climbing out of his Audi convertible and activating its hood. "That's a bit of luck so I can introduce you to him now," said Hannah. Bob, instantly feeling highly embarrassed because he now felt so scruffy, wanted to decline but it was too late.

If the wealthy estate agent had noticed the off-duty chauffeur's appearance, then he certainly didn't show it and five minutes later, the two were still standing in the car park discussing the attributes of the classic Bentley. Hannah had already excused herself, saying she had to pop into the office on an errand for Heather, before going shopping and would meet him back at the car around 11am, which would give him enough time to have a good look around the market town, if that was OK.

By the time the two men had stopped chatting, it had been arranged that Bob would drive his Bentley over to Royston's place that evening to see his small classic collection and maybe stay for a barbecue and that he was welcome to bring a guest. "I'll ask Hannah and Heather if they'd like to come too," he'd said.

Royston Randall might have become a wealthy man but he was very much down to earth and friendly, thought Bob as he made his way slowly up the High Street keeping an eye open for Milton's, which he eventually found near the top and next to the offices of the Draymarket Gazette.

Proprietor Danny Milton, standing behind his classy new wood and glass counter, instantly clocked the tired state of his customer's attire and wasn't holding out much

hope for a good sale. Bob wandered along a couple of rails only to find that the price of casual clothes in this county menswear boutique were way beyond his customary price range. There was no one else in the shop, which didn't surprise him, once he'd established that the pair of casual trousers, he'd picked out were £175 and that shirts seemed to start at £85 with light sweaters being almost off his personal Richter scale. Had he'd not committed himself to buying some new things and had not been driven into Draymarket specifically for that purpose, he'd have turned around and walked right out again but he was now trapped into spending more money on clothes than he'd ever done in his whole life and he knew it. Yet somewhere deep in the recesses of his psyche a seismic change occurred Why shouldn't he treat himself to some smart new clothes instead of the cheap bottom of the range things that had always been his previous choice?
He deserved a treat, he thought, shrugging off his mother's programming about saving for rainy days and making do. He no longer needed to make do so why should he? It was as if some financial floodgate had suddenly swung open, washing away all his previous inhibitions. He deserved a treat and he was jolly well going to have one. Bob walked out of Milton's thirty

minutes later clutching several large up market carrier bags and leaving Danny Milton with a completely unexpected smile on his face.

As there was still half an hour to spare before meeting up with Heather, Bob wandered up and down the busy High Street and on impulse popped into the newsagents and picked up a copy of The Draymarket Gazette. If he was going to be around for a week, then he might as well find out what made the place tick.

There was a cafe opposite so he went in, ordered a coffee and sat down to read it. His mobile rang just as he was leaving. It was Annie saying she was going for a stroll around the green with Miss Charlotte and confirming that he could now turn up around 2pm and perhaps they might all go for a drive around the area. He wondered whether now was the time to mention the barbecue at Royston's, just in case she'd like to accompany him, but decided it was best to leave it until later.

Corinne and her team were busy preparing for the lunchtime service by the time Annie and Miss Charlotte stepped out onto the green.

It was a glorious late morning with a series of small fluffy white clouds moving lazily across an otherwise clear blue sky. Charlie had spent the previous night thinking about Corinne, wondering what had become of Laura, the child she'd given away soon after birth, and recalling memories from her earlier life, which still stood out vividly like jagged rocks in a misty sea. She'd eventually fallen asleep only to slip into a series of troubled dreams but the sunlight streaming in through the curtains when she woke, quickly dispelled her sombre mood and lifted her spirits.

"You know Annie I do appreciate all you are doing for me," she said after they'd crossed the green to a seat and had sat in a companionable silence for a few moments. "You've always been my favourite ever since you arrived at Ocean View," she explained. "It's very kind of you to say that but it's always a pleasure to be in your company.

 I had a nice chat with the manager, who checked us in, and it turns out that her twin sister and husband live in that big house next door and that both their children help out when they're around. Come to think of it, that helpful young man who was watering the hanging baskets when we arrived must have been their son!"

 It was such an innocent statement, but the shock wave of emotion that swept over Charlie would have easily been enough to trigger a heart attack in a woman of a frailer constitution. Annie glanced across at her, instantly noticing the strange look that had suddenly transfixed her face.

"Are you all right?"

There was a long pause as Charlie grappled to come to terms with the shock news, her feelings now struggling between an immense joy that all that was lost had somehow been miraculously found, and an overwhelming desire to weep. Not only had she found her daughters but she also had grandchildren too!

"Look, my dear. Would you mind going for a little stroll by yourself, because I think I'd like to be on my own for a few minutes." Annie said she'd go and have a look around the church, whose steeple she could see above the trees. What could she possibly have said that had had such a profound effect on Miss Charlotte? she wondered, thinking back over their conversation.

Chapter 6

It was a sunny spring morning when the young woman said her family farewells, hefted a bulging rucksack onto her slim shoulders and set out from the rectory in Little Oreford. Two long country bus rides later she'd arrived in Exeter and boarded a train for Reading and thence on to Gatwick Airport to catch a flight out to the Caribbean and a completely new life as crew for one of the sailing-holiday companies. She'd learned both to sail on the waters of south Devon coast and to surf much closer to home on the rugged beaches of North Devon.
When the season came to a close, she didn't have any desire whatsoever to return to the restrictive and deadly dull life of her father's rectory, so she used the cash and the substantial tips she'd saved to go off travelling around central and south America, a pattern she repeated for the next three years until finally, after a particularly heart-rending break up with a lover, whom she firmly believed she would be with for life, she suddenly decided it was time to go home.
Jumping out of the frying pan and into the fire didn't come close to describing her feelings within a couple of weeks of returning to Albany House but where was she to go and just what should she to do next. Luckily her

childhood friend Robin Lloyd was back in the village visiting his parents, who lived in a chocolate box cottage beside the green.

It was over a pint at the Village's Oreford Inn, which seemed as if it was just about on its last legs, that he suggested she might enrol as a student at some university and obtain a degree in some practical discipline that might lead to a career.

It had driven Charlie's long-suffering parents mad that she never seemed to be doing any work at the expensive girls' school they scrimped to send her too but when it came to her exams, she gained several distinctions and then to their dismay she'd thrown it all away by going off to the Caribbean to become a sea gypsy, as far as they were concerned.

Going to university to make up for her wasted years appealed to Charlie who was now in search of a new direction and in no time at all she'd signed up for an economics degree at Bristol, after all as Robin had advised, she needed to gain some practical skill.

Again, she sat idly watched the countryside skip by on her bus journeys back to Exeter station to board a train, this time for Bristol Temple Meads. Thinking back over the past few weeks and the seeming indifference her father, the Rev Will Potter and her mother and indeed that of her older sister, Cynthia had shown towards her on her leaving home for the second time, made her feel sad.

It was as if they couldn't wait to see the back of her, which also made her feel angry at pretty much the same time. Still, that was all behind her now. She was going to have ball and finding a bed mate, was high on the list.

The trouble was that Charlie Potter had been the proverbial cuckoo in the family nest, almost from birth. Both her long-suffering parents and her sister were reserved, conventional people of moderate intelligence, who held their position as pillars of the local community in high regard and generally took life seriously. She, by complete contrast, was exceedingly bright, quick-witted and highly extrovert and that cocktail of qualities put her on an inevitable collision course with the rest of her family long before she was five.

The trouble was that the Rev Will Potter's youngest daughter could nearly always get the better of him in an argument from quite a young age and was both disobedient, a cardinal sin in his and his wife Anne's eyes, and wilful.

By the time she was ten, they'd completely given up trying to make her conform to their idea of how a country clergyman's daughter should behave and had reached an uneasy truce which allowed her to more or less ' run wild,' as they put it, with her best friends Margo and Robin Lloyd. Their parents, both academics, were far more laid back and thought nothing of allowing their children and Charlie to spend their free time, building dens, climbing trees and generally roaming together around the neighbouring countryside. This wasn't 'running wild' in their eyes; it was just kids enjoying themselves.The Lloyds' home was always in a constant muddle, in total contrast to the vicarage where everything was in its place and cleanliness was next to Godliness, so Charlie spent much of her time there and was more or less counted as an extra member of their family.

But all that was finally behind her now and she was looking forward to arriving in Bristol, checking in to a hall of residence near the university, which she'd visited briefly on a show around earlier that summer, and finding a fellow student willing to go out for a beer. She'd surprised her parents by achieving a combination of A and A stars in virtually all her A levels, despite seeming to have spent little time on revision, and Will Potter found himself in the strange position of actually feeling quite proud of his errant daughter's academic achievements. He casually mentioned her success in passing to several members of his inner circle within the local church going community and even suggested she might try for Oxford or Cambridge, but jetting off to crew in the Caribbean had far more appeal.

Her three years studying economics at Bristol passed in a haze of parties, drinking sessions in the pubs around fashionable and leafy Clifton and discussions long into the night on the pressing issues of the day, so when it came to finals time, the best she achieved was a second-class degree.

She'd managed fleeting visits back home but because both Robin and Margo had left to pursue careers in London, there was nothing for her in Little Oreford, so after a few uncomfortable days during which she and her family tolerated one another, she headed back to Bristol or to places where various friends were hanging out during the long vacations.

To start with, lack of money was a constant problem but all that changed one afternoon with a chance encounter on the city's College Green close to the cathedral.

She was strolling across the grass on her way to meet some friends in a nearby cafe when a well-dressed middle-aged couple stopped her to seek directions to the city's famous Cabot Tower. They were Americans, whose great grandparents had emigrated from the West

Country, and were on the customary, 'discover our roots' whistle-stop tour.

"That's a coincidence because I'm really interested in the city's history and I was up at the tower only yesterday so I could show you the way if you like," she heard herself say. It was true she had climbed the tower for a bird's eye view over Bristol, but wasn't the slightest bit interested in its history. Still, she'd read a leaflet about it and with her gift of an almost photographic memory, had retained most of the historical facts.

One thing led to another with the result that she spent the next couple of days showing the couple around, reading up on the city's social and economic history at night, which she actually found quite interesting, and skipping a couple of lectures to be their guide. The couple, who'd been staying at the city's fashionable Star Hotel, moved on but not before inviting her to come and stay should she ever find herself in Boston, paying her a fat tip and, best of all, recommending her services to George O'Brian, the hotel concierge, to whom she'd chatted, when going to collect them from the foyer. Charlie got friendly with George, who in exchange for a tip, would recommend her services to guests. She'd call him from a payphone in the university every couple of days to see if 'anyone was about,' as she put it.

George O'Brian, whose family had emigrated from Ireland to escape the great potato famine, was well over six foot and reed-thin, so much so, that his smart black and gold trimmed livery had to be specially made for him and when wearing his customary black bowler, he reminded Charlie of some comic Dickensian character. But he had a sharp memory for names and faces and when former guests returned, even after several years, he would greet them by name and welcome them back which made them feel special and was acknowledged and appreciated by successive general managers Charlie soon found she was enjoying her casual tourist encounters, so much so, that the number of skipped lectures increased until it reached a point where she was threatened with being 'sent down.' After that her attendances improved until the point was reached when she felt she could take a few more liberties with her long-suffering tutors. The annoying thing was that when Charlie engaged with them and her fellow students, her keen intellect and outgoing personality meant she was a real asset to the group and they tended to overlook her disappearances as long as she completed her study assignments which she usually did.

It was after taking her finals and finding out that she'd not done particularly well, that she turned up at The Star one morning.

On her stroll down fashionable Park Street with its array of upmarket shops and eateries, she'd decided to stick around Bristol for a while and build up some funds to go travelling.

She was now staying with a fellow student whose wealthy parents had brought her a small flat because she planned to stay on in the city and do a PhD so accommodation was not a problem.

George was busy loading cases into the boot of a taxi when she arrived at the hotel so she hung back waiting for him to complete the task before approaching. " Morning, Miss. The gent's waiting for you in the window seat just inside the coffee shop."

They'd now known one another for over two years but he still called her 'Miss' even though she'd long since asked him to use her name. "Oh no, Miss. What would my Corinne say if she found out I was being familiar with attractive young ladies?" Corinne, of course, knew all about Charlie and her unofficial guiding activities and Charlie knew all about her because after a few months she'd badgered her husband into inviting the young lady back to tea at their end of terrace semi in Bedminster on a Sunday afternoon.

They'd hit it off at once. Corinne, who to Charlie's surprise and silent amusement, could not have been much over five-foot tall, was homely, uncomplicated and everything that her own mother was not so the afternoon teas became a regular feature in Charlie's university life and as time went on, the childless couple began regarding her as the daughter they'd never had. Occasionally, small feelings of guilt would seep into Charlie's mind as she walked home from, what had now become supper rather than afternoon tea, because she now felt closer to Corinne than she ever had towards her own mother.

Somehow that didn't seem right because there had been the occasional times when their relationship seemed to warm, but then quickly cooled again. So what was making her mother tick? she wondered, and should she really start trying to understand her? Next time she was home she'd really make a big effort, she told herself but like all her many other good intentions that was to never happen.

The 'gent' waiting in the hotel coffee shop turned out to be a tanned and extremely good-looking and about her own age and way outside her normal middle to upper age clientele. What would a young guy like that want a guide for? Warning bells had started ringing even as she walked towards him.

Chapter 7

Annie was deep in thought as she wandered down the drive towards the door of St Michael's Church, Little Oreford. The beech trees on either side were now in full bright green leaf, although there were still a few tell-tale signs of the copper brown ones left over from the previous autumn, around the edges of the path.
What had she said that had had such a profound effect on Miss Charlotte? She started going back over their conversation in her mind but then her thoughts were interrupted by the mobile ringing in her pocket. "Hi Annie. How's it all going there?" asked Bob. She told him what had just happened. "Sounds a bit odd to me but maybe returning to her roots has thrown up some uncomfortable stuff from her past." His intuitiveness slightly surprised and impressed her. There was obviously more to Bob than she'd first appreciated. Of course, that was probably the answer so why hadn't she thought of that?
"The reason for the call is that I've been invited out to a barbecue this evening with a fellow car enthusiast I've just met and I thought I'd ask you now if you'd like to come too rather than spring it on you this afternoon." He was crossing his fingers that she'd agree. "It's nice of

you to ask Bob but I'm not sure I should just go off and leave Miss Charlotte on her own so I'll let you know later if that's OK." Now what was she do?

It would be great to go off with Bob for the evening and meet new people but the responsible professional in her was not so sure because what if Miss Charlotte became ill or suddenly needed her and she was out enjoying herself?

She sat in a pew at the back of the lofty and silent nave, watching the dust swirling around in a sudden shaft of light pouring in through one of the centuries old stained-glass windows. The answer, she told herself after wrestling with her conscience for a few minutes, was to ask her if she would mind and if she didn't, then to leave a telephone number to be called in case of an emergency because she and Bob were bound to be only a short distance away.

As she'd suspected, Charlie didn't mind in the slightest and whatever had been troubling her seemed to have passed by the time she re-joined her on the green. To her surprise, Charlie said she'd visit the church another time and maybe they should stroll back to the inn for lunch because it was now past noon and she was feeling quite peckish having not felt like much breakfast.

By the time Bob arrived, Charlie had gone up to her room to rest, saying she'd hardly slept a wink all night and was probably going to have a quiet afternoon but maybe they might go out for a short drive later. "Seems like there's nothing for it but to make ourselves comfortable in the bar or out in the courtyard and await further instructions," he suggested. The geranium-filled cobbled courtyard was in full sun, but one table was in a shady spot, so they sat down and ordered pints of lime and soda.

"That was very intuitive of you to suggest that Miss Charlotte might have been dwelling on some uncomfortable happening from her past when you called me this morning," said Annie. "Not really because when you think about it, to suddenly return to your childhood roots after a lifetime and to remember your parents, now both long gone, and to maybe realise that you won't be long in following them, must be quite thought provoking," he suggested. "We'll never know if you're on the right track or not, but Miss Charlotte's normally so full of life and interested in everything and I'm not sure she'd have morose thoughts like that. Just look at the way she stepped in and opened that village fete. I just couldn't believe that was actually happening, could you?" They laughed, both realising they were savouring a shared experience and finding enjoyment in one another's company.

Bob said they knew absolutely nothing about Miss Charlotte's childhood associations with Little Oreford and wondered whether they should maybe ask her at some appropriate time. "I don't really think that's a good idea, seeing she's instructed us not to mention that to anyone. She's always been very secretive about her past life. We've spent many an afternoon walking up and down the prom at home but never once had she talked about her previous life and I somehow felt in wasn't up to me to ask. It was only a few weeks ago that, right out of the blue, she suggested we should come here."

Their conversation was suddenly interrupted by her appearance. "I seem to have recovered, so shall we go for that drive now and maybe we'll have another little adventure like yesterday."

Annie and Bob looked at one another both wondering if 'having another little adventure' was really such a good idea. "You can sit in the front if you like, Annie, because it will give me more space to look around as we drive," she suggested. They both knew this was another blatant set-up, but neither resisted the suggestion.

"There's a little place near here called Yardley Upton and my friends and I would often walk down through the fields to buy sweets because it was our nearest village shop so maybe we could drive there and have a little stroll around."

While it was only a twenty-minute walk to Yardley, the drive took much longer because they'd not gone far through the narrow country lanes when they hit a 'diverted traffic' sign and then got stuck behind a lumbering farm vehicle. It had become strangely quiet in the back compared with the previous afternoon when Charlie had kept up a more or less continuous commentary. Annie glanced around fully expecting to find she'd drifted off to sleep but no she had not and was clearly deep in thought judging by the morose look on her face.

"Here we are then," announced Bob, who'd spent much of the journey resisting the ridiculous temptation to slide his left hand across and place it on Annie's exposed knee. They drove slowly into the centre of the village with Bob on full alert looking for somewhere to park. "Oh! my goodness. Look the village shop, it's still there after all these years; and The Black Swan too where I used to go with my friends and their parents and have orange squash and a packet of crisps in the garden at the back." Charlie was now back to her usual animated self and that was something of a relief, thought Annie. Bob drove past the pub and pulled into the village hall car park and they all got out.

"I must go into the shop and buy some chocolate or sweets for old time's sake. I haven't eaten them for years, but you two can have them." Annie and Bob exchanged 'here we go again' looks. "You two go on in. I'll just clean off the dust we seem to have accumulated from following that farm vehicle."

Annie glanced back at him as Charlie headed purposely towards a door, plastered with village notices, and gave him a look that said he'd got out of that one nicely.

The shop was surprisingly large inside because the young couple, who'd taken it over a year earlier, had carried out extensive alterations to what had formerly been an old house so that it now covered the whole ground floor and had been transformed into a mini supermarket. They'd also successfully applied and reopened the post office to the delight of villagers. A buzzer announced their arrival and alerted the young woman who popped out from behind the shelves she'd been on her knees restacking in a quiet moment.

"My goodness, this place was tiny in my day with hardly enough room to swing a cat and what's happened to that bell that used to jangle because it was attached to the door by a string?" asked Charlie. The woman said the bell had long gone but that she remembered it too from the days when her grandparents ran the shop. "Good gracious that was Mr and Mrs Cummings then. I think his name was Tom, wasn't it?"

Now she had the woman's full attention. "You're right. Tom and Agnes were my grandparents. How amazing that you should come in again after all these years. I can hardly believe it," she exclaimed. "I don't suppose you have a picture of them and the shop in those days? asked Charlie. "I can do better than that. I have a whole family album!" It was at that moment that the woman's husband emerged. "Oh! here's Richard and I'm Megan Brown by the way."

Five minutes later Bob, who'd been called in, found himself sitting with Annie and Miss Charlotte in the back garden while Megan went to make some tea and to return with her treasured album. Bob glanced at Annie and nodded his head as if to say he couldn't believe what was happening all over again. Charlie didn't notice because she was suddenly deep in thought with little internal warning bells ringing. She'd have to be very careful because this young woman would be sure to ask her about her childhood and if she explained in front of Annie and Bob that she was the former rector's daughter, then they would be bound to start asking her about her childhood and one thing might lead on to another. 'Will you ever learn to stop being so hasty,' she chided herself. Had she not discovered her twins were back in the village and that one of her daughters and her two grandchildren were actually living in Albany House, then she didn't suppose it would really have mattered but now it did matter and it mattered a lot. For she was still to make up her mind whether or not to reveal later in the week that she was the mother who'd abandoned them!

They stayed for nearly an hour and learned how, most unusually, the Yardley Upton village shop had stayed in the same family for around ninety years and now looked set to go on doing so for many more to come. Charlie's instincts had been right because Megan, who also turned out to be the Yardley Upton and Little Oreford Parish Council clerk, was keenly interested in local history and was anxious to know what her surprise customer could tell her about her childhood in the village.

Put on the spot, Charlie had talked in general terms about the village in those days and of her childhood memories of the surrounding area, but succeeded in managing not to mention she was the rector's daughter.

Annie was thinking about their surprise afternoon tea party on the drive back and it had not escaped her attention that Miss Charlotte had made no reference to her own family so was there an ulterior reason for that, she wondered.

Chapter 8

The smart but casually dressed young man rose from the coffee table as he spotted this extremely attractive young woman walking purposely towards him, a slightly puzzled look on her face. "Are you Charlie, because if so I'm Brad," he said in a voice she found friendly and instantly reassuring. "Do we have time for a coffee or are you keen to get going?" he asked. Charlie said 'yes' to a coffee because she'd had a late night, overslept and had left the flat in a hurry without any breakfast and besides it would be sensible to find out a little more about this man before setting out with him.

"George, the concierge, says you're quite the best guide in the city," Brad said conversationally as he waved her in to the seat opposite. "I wouldn't say that was true but might I be really straight and ask why you would want a guide when you certainly look the type who could quite easily navigate yourself around the city with one of the street maps that are over there on reception and the guide book that goes with it?" That's easy. I'm taking a day off after completing some fairly complex business negotiations and before flying home tomorrow. My brain needs a break and besides that, quite honestly, it would be nice to have some company."

The unexpectedly polite directness of his reply, embarrassed Charlie. "I hope you don't think me rude for asking," she replied, feeling her cheeks flushing. "Not at all. You were just being sensible, as anyone else in your position would have been," he replied evenly. "So what business are you in and where's home, if you don't mind me asking?"

Brad Meyer, she learned, was in the Canadian international financial investment sector and would be flying from Bristol to Amsterdam the following morning to pick up a flight back to Toronto. So why was his business not in London rather than the provincial city of Bristol, she wondered, but decided not to press it.

The three-hour morning tour turned into a magical and carefree whole day out, with a bistro lunch in fashionable Clifton and an afternoon at the city's colourful zoological gardens. Both now on a high, and he on a whim, stopping and looking into the window of a jeweller's shop, insisted on buying her a small silver St Christopher's medal on a chain as a keepsake. She protested but not terribly hard.

They were both single and had much in common. so much so that Charlie didn't want their day to end, so when he suggested supper in The Star's award-winning restaurant, she happily agreed. They'd earlier exchanged life stories and he'd suggested she might like to come out to Toronto where he'd be delighted to show her around his home 'town,' but clearly not as expertly as the tour he'd enjoyed today. She laughed at the intended compliment and told him not to say anymore because she might just take him up on his impromptu invitation. "No, seriously, I'm not joking and I really would like to see you again on my side of the pond," he said quietly, stretching out and taking her hand as he did so. Charlie made no attempt to draw it away and began thinking seriously about what she should do if he now suggested going upstairs to his room and spending the night together.

She knew instinctively this was most likely to be a one-night stand and was not really a good idea but she also knew that, despite any misgivings, she'd be unable to resist the invitation.

They did go upstairs with Charlie making sure she was not seen by any of the staff she'd got to know and making a mental note not to be spotted by George in the morning because that would definitely not be a good idea. No sooner had they closed the door then the hungry kissing began and their clothing torn off. It was if that with tomorrow's early morning parting, there wasn't a moment to be lost. There was an urgency to their love making, repeated in the early hours, with promises being made that it would not be long before they'd be together again because theirs was a shared chemistry that neither had ever experienced before.

There was absolutely nothing to prevent Charlie taking off for Canada because she was now foot lose and fancy free and before they'd torn themselves apart for the last time, she'd taken all his contact details and he hers and he'd promised to mail her an air ticket just as soon as he could.

Her day with Brad remained constantly in Charlie's thoughts over the next fortnight and she daily expected the arrival of her ticket. She'd resisted calling him for a couple of days but when she did, her excitement was quickly quelled by an answer phone. She tried again the following evening with her excitement still undiminished but again she was greeted by the same impersonal electronic 'not at home' message. Maybe he'd flown off on another assignment at short notice but had already put her ticket in the post, she rationalised.

But as the days slipped by with no word or Canadian stamped envelope, the reality that this really had been just a one-night stand and that he'd had absolutely no intention of seeing her again, had to be faced.

"You can't trust bloody men," her feminist flat-mate, Kate, had consoled her once she'd given up all hope that she would ever hear from Brad again. Autumn was sliding into winter, George's supply of guests looking to be shown around the city had almost dried up and after the Brad affair, her heart had gone out of the enterprise anyway.

"You need a new challenge, Charlie. Maybe something in local tourism where you now have a bit of a track record," Kate suggested after they'd both toasted a 'sod off' to Brad' where ever he was. The suggestion hit an optimistic chord and Charlie threw herself enthusiastically into job hunting mode as a way of kick-starting her life again and eventually landed a sales and part operational role with a young regional event management company. She had lots of ideas and loads of enthusiasm and quickly made herself a valuable part of the company's small hands-on team.

It had just begun to seem to Charlie that she'd at last turned her life around when the bouts of morning sickness started and, although she remained in denial for several weeks, she eventually forced herself to face up to the fact that she just might be pregnant! A doctor's appointment confirmed that she was indeed three months gone.

Brad's baby, she had absolutely no doubt that it was his, would duly arrive the following June.

Her flatmate Kate was certainly underwhelmed at the prospect of having a baby around the place as was made blatantly clear by her half-hearted congratulations, so what the hell was she going to do now?

Chapter 9

By the time Annie and Bob arrived back at The Oreford Inn with Charlie, it had been agreed that Bob would take tea with her in the small guest lounge while she went up to change for their barbecue evening out together. Being a late Monday afternoon, it was quiet and Bob couldn't help feeling a little self-conscious sitting there in his Chauffeur's uniform sipping tea from a dainty cup but Charlie was enjoying the experience of having him all to herself for a while. She gently quizzed him about his life and he quickly realised she was a good listener and extremely easy to talk to. He even reached the point of telling her about that morning's clothes shopping expedition but something made him draw back.

Up in her room just over their heads, Annie was in a dilemma over what she should choose from her extremely limited wardrobe. When she'd packed for the trip, the idea of attending a summer evening barbecue at the residence of a clearly wealthy estate agent could not have been further from her thoughts.

As the weather was settled and it looked all set for a warm evening, she chose a blue skirt and matching blouse and not the casual jeans that had been her only other practical choice, but she decided to take a sweater just in case it got chilly late.

Bob looked up appreciatively as she entered the room and was quickly on his feet and thinking how attractive she looked.

"Now you young people, go off and enjoy yourselves and don't worry about me because I'm going to sit here for a while and have some supper sent up to my room later." Not long after they'd left, Corinne Potter put her head around the door to ask if they wanted anymore tea. "Oh! your chauffeur's left. I didn't see him go," she exclaimed. "Yes, he and my companion have gone off for the evening, but I'm glad I've seen you because I was wondering if I might have a little supper in my room later." Corinne said she go and find a menu.

Having just that brief moment with her unsuspecting daughter sent Charlie's emotions into a spin. Should she engage her in conversation and try and learn a little more about her life and that of Laura's and how they'd both ended up in Little Oreford? she agonised. No, it would be far better to say nothing until she'd found an innocent way of meeting Laura and maybe getting to look around Albany House, she decided. But on her way back to the lounge with the menu, Corinne had made up her mind that she wanted to know a little more about her chauffeur and companion accompanied elderly guest. She had a few minutes to spare before her deputy Flora took over for the evening, so she would stay for a chat. "So, what brings you to Little Oreford, Mrs Edwards?" she inquired brightly. The use of her surname reassured Charlie, because Annie would have signed her in as Mrs C Edwards and there really was no reason why her true identity should be revealed. "I've always loved the softness of North Devon, so different from the years spent with my late husband in the Caribbean before retiring to the south coast after his death.

"I decided that a little tour around this part of the world would be nice.

"Annie tells me you're rather one big happy family and that your sister and brother-in-law live in the big house next door and that you run this lovely inn with your nephew and niece helping out in their spare time," she probed. "Yes, that's right. I'm in charge here while my sister and her husband, Ben, run The Old Mill House craft and artisan workshops on the far end of the green, near the church." Charlie said they sounded most interesting. Are visitor's welcome?" she asked. "Very definitely so because there's a shop where you can buy a whole range of things made from wood, metals and other materials, as well as hand-weaved scarves and jewellery. The old mill machinery is still there and has been made rather a feature with a special exhibition area." "Goodness how did Annie miss all that when she walked over to the church this morning? Charlie wondered. "Probably because it's open at weekends and closed on Mondays," said Corinne, who suddenly heard the reception telephone ringing and said that she'd better go and answer it The caller was Annie, apologising for forgetting to leave both their telephone numbers in case there was an emergency involving Mrs Andrews.

"So, what's the plan Bob?" she'd asked as they they'd driven away from Little Oreford. "We're going back to my B&B so that I can change and then my host Hannah is going to come with us to show us the way while her partner Heather follows in her car.

"Oh! so we're all going!" she said. "That's right because it turns out they're great friends with Royston Randall and his wife, Alicia, and worked in his Hampton Green agency before he expanded into Draymarket and they're both still involved with the business.

Bob looked down, catching a tantalising glimpse of Annie's exposed left knee and discreetly averted his gaze, but this small attention had not escaped her and, to her surprise, she felt flattered and inclined to let her skirt ride a little higher. She was really looking forward to their evening and had made up her mind that she was going to have a good time.

Hannah and Heather welcomed her into their lounge, as if she was some long-lost friend, while Bob went up to change. He hadn't mentioned his shopping expedition to Annie but she quickly learned about it from his hosts, who were now treating him more like a younger brother rather than their paying guest.

The Randall residence was a substantial Victorian mansion on higher and lightly wooded ground overlooking Draymarket. It was reached by a private drive, winding its way up through manicured lawns to emerge onto a wide turning circle in front of the house. Royston and Alicia were out on the entrance porch steps to greet them because they'd asked Anthony, their nine-year-old, to keep an eye open for the Bentley.

"Is this going to be another car for your collection, Dad?" the lad asked as the motor drew to a halt in front of them with Heather's car now close behind it. But his question went unanswered as the couple stepped forward to welcome their guests. Both Annie and Bob suddenly felt out of their depth, but were quickly made to feel completely at ease by their hosts and by Heather and

Hannah, who obviously had the run of the place and were clearly more close friends than employees.

"Come and have a look at my motors, Bob. Do you want to come too, Annie?" Royston asked.

"I think that's more boys' toys so perhaps you could show me around your lovely garden, Alicia." Hannah and Heather said they'd been around the garden lots of times so they'd go and find a glass of wine and sit on the patio and enjoy the last of the evening sun seeing their godson had gone off with his dad and Bob.

"Do you have a garden, Annie?" Alicia asked, having left her briefly to return with two large flutes of sparkling white wine. "No, but my parents do and they're great gardeners, so I guess some of their enthusiasm has just rubbed off on me." The two talked about the plants and shrubs as they walked around the grounds and briefly exchanging life stories.

Annie learned how Alicia had come to Hampton Green to teach at the village school some years earlier and had met Royston, Heather and Hannah when she'd rented a property in the village. "You all seem very close if you don't mind me saying so," she observed. "We're certainly that. Royston gave the girls a stake in his business when he bought out a rival agency in Draymarket which was the start of their expansion."

"But look, can you excuse me because I'd better go back and get supper organised. It was going to be a barbecue. but it's a buffet instead. I hope that's all right."
No sooner had she disappeared into the house and before Annie could go in search of the others, another car pulled up outside the house and a middle aged, smartly dressed woman got out. "Hello, I'm so sorry I'm late, yet again," she said advancing on Annie
"I'm Jackie Benson, Editor of the Draymarket Gazette, so where is everybody?"
Annie introduced herself, saying that Alicia had just gone into the house to see about supper and that Royston and her companion Bob were looking at his car collection.
"Sounds par for the course," Jackie replied.

The buffet supper was laid out on a grand table in a large Victorian drawing room and during the course of the evening, Annie and Bob learned that Royston and Jackie Benson were joint trustees of The Draymarket Gazette Trust, established by a former proprietor to ensure the paper remained independent.

There was no emergency call from The Oreford Inn and it was approaching midnight when the Bentley finally drove away from the house with Hannah, Heather and Annie in the back because they'd all had a little too much to drink.

It had surprised Bob that Annie hadn't chosen to sit in the front with him. It had been a really great evening up until then but now he felt mildly upset and just a little confused. He was driving directly to Little Oreford to drop her off so would not be having any time on his own with her.

The three were keeping up a steady stream of chatter about the evening and occasionally including him in the conversation but it was clear they were all a little worse for wear. Annie was woozy, warm and comfortable, lounging in semi darkness on the soft leather seats with the faint smell of polish in the air and feeling literally on top of the world. It had been a great evening and she'd really let her hair down with Heather and Hannah for the first time in years.

Then her thoughts turned to Bob, all by himself in the front and suddenly felt a tinge of guilt that she hadn't climbed in beside him. She really did like Bob, she decided.

Back at The Oreford, he escorted her inside, thinking the place might be in darkness, but there were lights on and people still about. "Thanks, Bob. I'll be OK from here and I'll call you in the morning" she said giving him a smile and a gentle squeeze on the arm that was some consolation. Returning to the car, he found Hannah sitting in the front passenger seat! "We rather felt we'd been ignoring you, so I thought I'd keep you company on the drive home" she said.

Chapter 10

All Charlie's close university friends had left Bristol in pursuit of their careers or to take gap years before returning to study for higher degrees, so she felt utterly alone, apart from her work friends who were either married or in long term relationships. There was nothing for it, she'd just have to go home for the weekend and break the news to her parents and she could just imagine their recriminations. She knew it was going to be a nightmare and it was exactly that. She told them over breakfast, having spent a troubled night in her old room and had left by lunchtime telling them they'd never see her again which gave her just a crumb of satisfaction.

After she'd gone, the Rev and Mrs Potter and her sister Cynthia took Charlie at her word and closed the book on her because they knew she meant what she'd said. Charlie was never spoken of again under the roof of Albany House, but completely unknown to each other, both her parents secretly prayed for her and for the grandchild they both knew they would probably never live to see. Charlie had been all that they were not, always needing to say just what she thought, while they had long since given up trying to really talk to one

another. Both had the perfect excuse being kept busy tending and giving support and bringing comfort to their ever-dwindling flock who thought the world of them. The only one who really knew what was going on was their long-time home-help and herself a very private person. Only once was she heard to remark to one of her few friends, who was a little in awe of the Rev and Mrs Potter, that 'street angels could often be house devils!'
On the journey back to Bristol, Charlie began facing up to the fact that there was only one couple she could really turn to in her hour of need and that was George and Corinne. She'd so wanted to avoid involving them, but now she realised she really had no alternative. She was due to have supper with them the following Friday so she'd leave it until then.

Back home she'd put in another call to Brad, but this time the line was dead. The week passed quickly enough with preparation for an outside event in the grounds of Ashton Court Park, on the edge of the city and it was as they were packing up after work on the Wednesday that she'd decided to tell her boss that she was pregnant because there didn't really seem any point in keeping it a secret any longer. There were congratulations all round and promises of support, but it was a very small outfit and she knew she'd simply leave when the time came and probably not return at the end of her statuary maternity period.

Breaking the news to George and Corinne after supper had been one of the hardest things she'd ever done. She'd always given them the impression she was full of confidence and enjoying life and her new career, but now she actually felt very alone and extremely vulnerable. When the tears started flowing down her cheeks, Corinne was around the table in an instant and giving her a hug, while George who was sitting next to her reached across and put a long and protective arm around her shoulder. "Don't worry dear. We'll look after you when your time comes won't we, George?" she said. "Oh! I was so hoping you'd say that," Charlie sobbed. By the time she'd hugged them both goodbye it had been arranged that she'd move in with them when she was seven months pregnant and that nothing would give them greater pleasure than preparing a room for the baby. "Charlie's been like the daughter we've never had and now we're going to have a grandchild, so we're well and truly blessed George," said Corinne.

But sadly it was never to be. George had not been feeling well of late. He'd developed a dry cough and had started feeling a little breathless after handling not even the heaviest piece of the luggage at work. He was now nearing sixty and was bound to be slowing up, he rationalised and in typical man fashion, had kept this to himself, but then when he'd started feeling out of breath while climbing the stairs at night, he knew something was wrong.

A visit to their family doctor and few weeks spent on referrals followed by a chest x-ray confirmed what they'd secretly dreaded, that George had developed lung cancer and probably had less than two years to live. They broke the news to Charlie over supper and all three ended up hugging and in tears. "We still want you to come here before you have the baby and we want that more than anything don't we George? And besides that, it will help to take our minds of all of this horridness," said Corinne.

But as the weeks passed, George's condition deteriorated faster than expected until the point came when they all three realised that for Charlie to have her baby and bring it home to them was really not going to be possible.

How cruel could life be. Just a couple of months earlier, all seemed to be looking up.

Staying with George and Corinne before and then after the birth had seemed the perfect solution, especially as she'd realised just how much happiness that would have brought into the lives of her dear friends. Now all had been snatched away and she was once again almost totally alone in the world, and not having a clue as to what on earth to do for the best.

Chapter 11

Annie climbed into bed still feeing woozy and immediately fell asleep. It was getting on for 7.30am when, sunlight streaming through the curtains, finally woke her. She lay there for a few moments in that warm and comfortable space on the surface of consciousness and began thinking about Bob and that she would start a relationship with him if that's what he wanted.

She dressed and went across the hallway and tapped on Miss Charlotte's door. She found her sitting up in bed. "Oh! I'm glad you've come, because it's another lovely sunny morning and just perfect for you and Bob to go off and enjoy a ride out together."

It was if Miss Charlotte had been reading her thoughts. "But what will you do? "she asked, "That's easy because the old mill at the other end of the green is full of craft workshops where visitors are free to wander around and watch people making things so I'll spend lots of time in there. We didn't notice it yesterday because it's closed on Mondays. So why don't you give Bob a call and when you go down perhaps you could ask them to send up a small portion of scrambled egg on toast and a pot of tea."Luckily Corinne was behind reception and promised that she and the rest of her team would keep a close eye on Mrs Andrews. "My brother-in-law Ben manages things over at the mill so I'll ask him to look out for her." Annie stepped out onto the green and called Bob who said he'd be up in an hour and had already come up with a plan for their tour. Corinne took Charlie's breakfast tray up herself.

She still felt there was something just a little intriguing about their clearly quite wealthy, guest who'd rolled into their world in a chauffeur-driven Bentley with a young companion and with no greater desire, it seemed, other than to be left to wander around their small village and visit the Old Mill.

"Now where would you like me to put the tray," she asked brightly. "Leave it on that small table next to the chair by the window and I can enjoy my breakfast looking out over the green." As she turned to leave the room, their eyes met and it seemed to Corinne that a look of entreaty had suddenly flickered across her face. "Are you all right, Mrs Andrews?" she aske. "Yes dear. I'm fine," she replied, but inside she was now feeling anything but fine as the painful memory of the day her six-month-old Corinne had also been given up for adoption.

She should never have come back to Little Oreford and left the past in the past where all the guilt and regret had been softened by the passage of time. It seemed impossible to believe that her twin daughters had both found their way back to the village where she was born and yet it had happened. Again, the positive side of her nature took over and she told herself for the umpteenth time just how incredibly blessed she'd been to have actually found her girls, whom by any law of chance she should never have seen again.

Corinne walked thoughtfully downstairs. She was still puzzled as to why Mrs Andrews had sent Annie and Bob off for the day and seemed only to want to stay and wander around the village.

It really didn't make a lot of sense, so what was going on?

She didn't normally take much notice of their guests and their holiday arrangements, but this was somehow different, she told herself as she picked up the phone and rang The Old Mill House to tell Ben about Mrs Andrews.

"I'll do my best to keep an eye on her but I'm going to be quite busy showing around a chap called Dan Smith. He works on a glossy magazine weekend supplement for one of the national papers and seems to have decided that we're just perfect for a travel piece featuring the Hidden Gems of North Devon. How he found out about us I haven't a clue, but it should be great publicity for us and for you because if we do get lots of extra visitors, they're sure to want to come in for lunch or afternoon tea," he reasoned. "That's really great and if he's got time to pop in for a complimentary lunch just send him on over. I'll reserve a nice table in the window just in case."

Charlie was still sitting by her bedroom window when the Bentley pulled up outside the inn and after a few minutes drove off again. Somehow seeing her 'minders' disappearing down the road and leaving her by herself with the freedom to do exactly what she wanted was deliciously liberating. 'I'm tired of all this room service,' she told herself, having discarded the half-eaten scrambled egg, 'so I shall dress and go down to the dining room for a coffee.'

The breakfast service was almost over by the time she entered the oak beamed dining room and sat down at a table by the window, the one that had earlier been occupied by Annie.

"Let me clear the table for you," offered a young voice, making Charlie, who'd been peering through the window, turn and look up into the fresh face of an extremely pretty girl.

"That would be very kind and who are you, my dear, because I've not seen you before, have I?" she asked. "That's easy. I'm Lottie. I live next door and my Aunt Corinne's the manager here and I've popped in to help out because she's a bit short staffed this morning." So, this was her granddaughter! Charlie could feel her heart begin to beat a little faster. "I suppose that nice young man watering the plants, who came over to help when we arrived on Sunday must have been your brother?" she asked, now almost certain she knew the answer. "Yes. That was Luke, but he's not around because he's gone off to the beach for a few days surfing with some friends, she explained. "Is that far?" asked Charlie, wanting to prolong the conversation and to keep up the pretence that she didn't know the area. "Did you get home all right Bob?" asked Annie. It was one of those meaningless conversational question just asked out of politeness, but his answer surprised her. "Yes, but when I got back to the car, Hannah had climbed into the front passenger seat and spent most of the journey with her head sagging on my shoulder" he revealed. "Really! I knew she was pretty tipsy, but I didn't think she was that far gone." replied Annie, now feeling a renewed tinge of guilt that she had not taken the seat beside him on the journey home. "So, what's your plan for the day then Bob?" she asked, in a bid to sweep away her guilt. "The Dartmoor National Park's not many miles from here and I once read that if you flew to the middle in a light-aircraft, you'd actually reach a point when you'd only see moorland in all directions.

"I don't know if that's true or not because I suppose it would depend on just how high you were flying, but ever since then I've thought I'd like to drive across it from one side to the other, but the opportunity has never arisen until now," he explained. "That's a great idea. I've never done that either, so what shall we do about lunch?" she asked. "We have two choices: Princetown and Two Bridges, which is a small place in the middle of the moor, both have places to eat, or we could stop in Tavistock on our side of the national park and buy a picnic and then we could stop wherever we wanted," he suggested. "That's a lovely idea but what time do you think we'd be back?" Annie asked, feeling a small tinge of excitement. "In plenty of time for you to say goodnight to the old girl," he responded. "But are you going to feel comfortable driving your beautiful car on possibly narrow roads across a lonely moor?" she asked. "I'm sure it'll be fine, but just think how dull life would be if we went through it always choosing the safest option."

The truth was that he'd always erred on the side of caution, but something deep in his psyche had changed the day he'd spent over £250 on new clothes to go to the barbecue and because he was to have a whole day out with Annie, now sitting by his side in her pretty blue summer dress.

Just maybe the reason he'd always pulled away from previous relationships when they'd started getting serious was not because he was frightened, but more because he realised that they weren't right, he told himself as they headed for Tavistock. But Annie was different and he really felt that he'd not hold back again if by any chance she fell for him too.

It was close to midday by the time they'd bought their sandwiches, bottles of water and two miniature bottles of sparkling wine and were heading up onto the moor.

"That wine's going to be lukewarm by the time we get around to drinking it," she observed. "No, it's not because I have a small fridge in the boot, which I installed so that wedded couples could have a little toast on their way from the church to their receptions," he revealed, "Don't tell me you also lay on canopies as well!" she replied. "I've certainly done that a number of times but mostly when driving small parties out to the theatre in Plymouth.

"Now we're a party of two," she said happily as they left the trees and emerged out onto open moorland with an empty road snaking its way ahead of them. Bob glanced across and returned her lovely smile. "I'm not going to hurry because there's lots of passing places and if traffic builds up behind us, then I'll just pull in and let them all fly past," said Bob who'd noticed a number of spots where they could pull off the road at viewpoints. Annie thought that was a good idea and that maybe they could walk away from the car and find a quite spot for their picnic.

"Did you know that in New Zealand, you have to pull in and let traffic pass if you start causing a tail-back?" she asked.

"What a sensible idea. How do you know that?" he enquired. "My aunt and uncle, mum's sister and her husband, sailed to Sydney on a £10 assisted package back in the days when they were encouraging emigration and I went out there for a long holiday when I was eighteen. They wanted me to apply to stay and I often wonder if I should have grasped the opportunity, but I guess, being an only child, I didn't want to desert my mum and dad, neither of whom were in the best of health."

He was tempted to say that if she'd stayed in New Zealand then they would never have met and would not be having this wonderful day together. 'Go on be brave and say it anyway,' a voice in his head demanded and before he knew it, he had. "That's a nice thing to say, Bob," she said, glancing across at him. "I seem to spend quite a lot of my time saying I should have done this or I should not have done that which, when you think about it, is a completely pointless exercise," he added.

"You and me both," said Annie. "So, give me a recent example if you can think of one," he challenged and the fact that she'd climbed into the back seat with Hannah and Heather last night immediately sprang into her mind. "Do you really want the very latest one?" she asked. "If you're happy to share it with me then I do," he said. She paused. "Well, last night I got into the back of your car with the others, when I really should have joined you in the front. It really was an unkind and unthinking thing to do and sort of demoted you to the role of chauffeur."

Now it was Bob's turn to decide whether to admit he had been hurt or simply to save her embarrassment by saying he hadn't given it a second thought.

But if he brushed it aside, it would have been to suggest that he was in some way superior to her, which he was not, so he told her the truth. "I was a little surprised because I had sort of been looking forward to the drive back to Little Oreford with you," he admitted quietly. "Well, you won't believe this, but I paid a price for my actions because Hannah, who'd had a lot more to drink than me, started coming on to me and caressing my right leg above the knee in the darkness!" she revealed. "Bloody hell, Annie, and I only got a loll on the shoulder. I wonder why?" Then they were both laughing.

Shortly afterwards, they found a spot to pull off the road, park the Bentley and stroll along a small animal track through the light undergrowth to a little rise with wide views over the rolling landscape and with a series of sharp outcrops of grey rock dotting the near horizon. "I think they must be the famous Dartmoor tors," said Bob. It was a good spot for their picnic because they could also keep an eye on the car so he went back to collect the basket he'd filled before they left Tavistock.

Unpacking their impromptu lunch, he also produced a guide to Dartmoor and handed it to her. "When did you pick that up? she asked, expressing her surprise. "I spotted it in the newsagents in Draymarket and it was what gave me the idea that we should come here."

Suddenly the throaty roar of engines rudely interrupted the moorland silence and they both turned towards the sound as first one and then a whole cavalcade of bikers burst upon the scene, their spotless machines gleaming in the sunshine.

They watched them go flashing by, but then the last two or three riders slowed, turned and came roaring back and swept into the parking area, attracted by the lone Bentley like bees to a black honey pot. Now, as if on some biker's instinct, the rest of the swarm were returning and sweeping into the car park.

Heart thumping, Bob was on his feet and running back down the track with Annie close on his heels. The bike tyres were already kicking up fine clouds of dust that would soon be all over his precious car.

As he approached, his emotions a heady mixture of fear and anger, the noise of the now idling engines, spluttered out as, one after another, the leather-clad riders removed their helmets and switched off.

Suddenly there was complete silence, the depth of it accentuated by what had gone before. "That's a mighty fine classic Bentley you've got there. I bet she's a smooth dream to drive." The appreciative and clearly knowledgeable comment came from the red leather-clad rider, the first to enter the car park. 'Yes, but now she's covered in dust thanks to you,' Bob was tempted to say, but his overwhelming relief that these guys appeared to be a friendly bunch, held his tongue. "Yes. She does handle rather well but she's a sedate old lady compared to your Harleys," replied Bob, who'd quickly clocked the famous American make of all the bikes now surrounding them. "That's not the point because, like our bikes, she's a beautifully engineered and you must spend a lot of hours keeping her in that condition. Mind if we take a look inside?" the biker asked, allowing his machine to rest over on its stand and slowly climbing off and, as if on cue, all the other riders, did the same.

For some reason Annie, who'd watched the whole scene unfold, standing supportively by Bob's side, suddenly thought of their half-unpacked lunch and said she'd go back and close the basket and maybe have a quick flick through their guide book.

It was a good half hour before the cavalcade finally roared out of the car park heading for Tavistock and Bob walked slowly back up the track carrying a large rug which he'd forgotten to unpack.

A bank of white fluffy clouds had stolen silently across the scene from the west, which was quite a relief because, it had started to become uncomfortably hot, Annie thought. The bikers, it seemed, were all from the South-east and members of a Harley Davidson Club on their annual summer tour.

"For a horrible moment, when we realized they'd seen the Bentley and were all coming back, I thought we were in trouble, but how wrong I was. Just shows how one shouldn't jump to conclusions," said Bob. "Yes, but you can't blame yourself for that because with all that noise, suddenly being confronted by a party of leather-clad and helmeted figures was pretty intimidating," she replied as they sat side by side eating their sandwiches. "Do you know what?" he said, suddenly turning towards her. "What," she replied. "I completely forgot to take our sparkling out of the fridge," he said, getting to his feet and starting to run back to the car. She followed his progress with an appreciative gaze. He really was a very nice man.

"Do you know something else," he said as they sat sipping their wine. "What else? she asked, wondering just what might be coming next. "Ever since those bikers left, not a single car has passed us by."

Now they were both concentrating on the road below and waiting expectantly but all remained silent and still. "I bet there's been an accident at one end of the road or the other and traffic is being diverted," he said, fishing out his mobile phone to call up their location but, as he'd half expected, there was no signal. Collecting his big road map from the car, he laid it out on the ground in front of him and began studying it.

They were only about half way towards the middle of the moor and it was now coming up to 3pm, according to his watch. "I don't think we're going to have time to complete the crossing today if we're going to get back to Little Oreford at a reasonable hour, so I guess we may as well go back from whence we came and maybe try again before we go home if there's the time and an opportunity," he suggested. "OK but let's have ten-minute snooze before we go," she said suddenly laying back on the rug and putting her hands behind her head. "Mind if I join you," he asked. "Of course not," she said, moving over from the middle of the rug. Her closeness excited him and was enough for now.

Shortly afterwards, the sound of a motor filled the silence and their heads pooped up, like two meerkats, to see a campervan coming towards them from the Tavistock direction. "Looks like the road's reopened, if it was ever closed, so I guess it's time to go," said Bob, lending her a hand to get to her feet. It happened.

They said little as they drove slowly back towards Tavistock, both being wrapped in their own thoughts. As soon as there were a couple of vehicles behind them, he pulled the big car in and allowed his followers to escape before they became frustrated and started tail gating him.

"It's amazing how different the views look when you're driving along the same road in the opposite direction," Annie remarked but his reply to her casual observation surprised her. "Maybe it's a bit like the situations that pop up and confront one in life because there's always more than one way of looking at them." "That's a bit profound for a lovely afternoon," she observed. There was a lot more depth to this man than first appeared and that was pleasing to her.

Driving slowly down into Tavistock, it soon became clear there had indeed been an accident because the road had now been reduced to a single lane with officers from two parked police cars, directing the traffic. "Oh my God, look over there," said Annie, as soon as they'd passed the obstruction, but Bob had already seen the mangled remains of a bike on the side of the road and the party of bikers all parked up and standing around their machines close by. "Are we going to stop Bob?" "I think so, don't you?" The bikers had also spotted the Bentley and a couple of them detached themselves from the group and walked over to explain what had happened. Peter, their friend in the red leathers, had been leading and, swerving to avoid a car that had suddenly pulled out in front of them, lost control of his machine, which slid across the road and smashed into a wall. He was OK, but in a bit of a mess and a couple of their friends had ridden off with the ambulance to the nearest A&E. Bob reached into a glove compartment and produced his business card. "We can't really stop now, but if there should be anything we can do to help then just give us a call," he offered.

Chapter 12

As Christmas approached, Charlie began having second thoughts about her vow never to return to Albany House. It would be a real climb down and she was not used to that, but then when she imagined the uncomfortable welcome she'd most likely receive, she felt even less inclined to go back on her resolve. It was now becoming obvious she was pregnant so how would her parents explain that to anyone who happened to notice and comment on it. No that would be all too embarrassing for them and for her so she wouldn't go home for Christmas, but she might give them a call, she thought, but one thing led to another and she never did.

Charlie had not been looking forward to the festivities, but in the end, she'd had a better time than she'd expected. Her flatmate was off home to her family, but said she could stay and look after the place, as long as there were no parties, and a couple of members of her group, who happened to live in and around the city, invited her to join in their festivities. They'd long ago discovered that Charlie's gregariousness and quick wits were an asset to any party. Outwardly she was the same old flirty, happy-go-lucky Charlie, but the festive veneer was little more than skin deep and inside she was troubled and unhappy.

Had her whole life been little more than an act, she pondered making her way slowly home from the pub late on Christmas Eve.

The wild childhood times she'd shared with Robin and Margo, her continued defiance of her long-suffering parents and her determination to always do what she wanted, just where had all that got her? She'd failed to achieve little more than a mediocre second-class degree when she knew she could have done so much better had she'd not wasted most of her three years, and now she was pregnant with no idea what to do next. But then the positive side of her nature began gently reasserting itself. No. it wasn't all an act. Her situation was the result of her personality and it had not all been a waste. She'd met dear George and Corinne to whom she felt so close and she was going to her utmost to give them the best Christmas day ever.

She and Corinne had moved the couple's spare bed down into their 'front room,' because George was beginning to find it a struggle climbing the stairs so they spent the day around their kitchen table, all doing their best to be happy with the assistance of an increasing amount of alcohol. "Let's face it. I've had it and I'm not going to see my darling girls anymore," said George over the ruins of his late afternoon turkey dinner. He'd wearied of pretending to be happy. "Charlie you've been a real little light in our lives and I want you to promise you'll always be there for Corinne." There were tears in his frightened eyes. "Oh George, of course we'll be there for each other won't we, Corinne?" promised Charlie, struggling to keep her own tears at bay.

George finally gave up the struggle on a bitterly cold February Monday afternoon with Corinne and Charlie by his side.

She had come to stay with the couple a few days earlier, sleeping on an air bed in their spare room.

"I think we should tell the manager at The Star because there's sure to be people who worked with George who'll want to come to the funeral," suggested Charlie. They were sitting at the kitchen table wrapped in the cold air of unreality after the local undertaker had departed.

George was to be buried in an overgrown family plot at the city's rambling Arno's Vale cemetery at noon the following Tuesday. "Would you like me to stay with you until after the funeral? If so, I'll pop back to the flat for a few more things and call in at The Star on my way back?" she offered. "Oh! Charlie, what would I do without you," said Corinne.

It felt really weird walking into the Georgian hotel's cool marble and chandeliered foyer and being greeted by a strange new doorman, who was as rotund as George had been tall. She recognised the smart blue-suited senior receptionist, who, like George, had been at her post for some years, because long-serving General Manager, Walter Williams, treated his team well. Minutes later she was being accompanied by the now grave faced woman in the lift and up to the GM's office where he was waiting to meet her at the door. They shook hands and he bade her take a seat on the small sofa where it was his custom to conduct more informal interviews over tea or a pot of coffee. "Don't I recognise you?" he asked after expressing his sadness at George's passing.

When Charlie had finished telling her story of how she came to meet George, the GM leaned back in his chair and gave her a searching look. "The Star could use a clearly bright young person like you if you were available for employment say next summer," he said seeing her condition.

"But you don't have to think about it now," he added, noting the shocked look of surprise on Charlie's face. "In the meantime, I hope George's widow will allow us to host a small farewell reception for him after the funeral as our mark of respect for his many years of loyal service."

There was only a small gathering for the funeral in the local Methodist Church and for the interment at the cemetery because the couple had few surviving relatives. But the General Manager and around twenty hotel team members were waiting quietly to offer their condolences at the wake, including some who'd changed shifts to be present or had come in on their days off. Corinne had tears in her eyes, being overwhelmed by the respect these kind people had for her beloved George. Standing close by, Charlie, was suddenly close to despair as she relived her sunny day of promise with Brad, their intimate dinner for two in the restaurant next door, their love making and his betrayal. Now six months pregnant, it had been agreed she'd give up her flat share and move in with Corinne at the end of March, but in the meantime, they'd begin decorating the smallest bedroom as a nursery. Arriving at Corinne's early one afternoon, weighed down with rolls of wallpaper and other decorating materials she was surprised by the unhappy look on her elderly friend's face.

"Are you OK?" she asked.

Following Corinne into the kitchen, she put down her heavy load and collapsed into a chair. "Not really, dear, because I received this letter yesterday," she said, sitting down at the kitchen table and handing an official-looking brown envelope to Charlie.

It was from the city council, whose records showed she was now a single woman living in a three-bedroom house and that as there was a severe shortage of family size homes, a housing officer would be calling to discuss her moving to a smaller and more suitable property.

"It's not fair. You've lost George and now you're going to lose your home as well," said Charlie, glancing down at the rolls of wallpaper so optimistically brought just a couple of hours before. Now what are we going to do?" she asked, suddenly feeling close to despair. "I know, dear, but I haven't really got a leg to stand on, have I?"

Gloria Summerfield, the middle-aged doctor in the family practice, established in a rambling four-storey house on a leafy tree-lined street in the fashionable Clifton area of Bristol, not far from where Charlie lived, had finished her examination. She knew her patient was going to be a single mum and over the space of several consultations, had learned a little of her story.

"I'm not quite sure how you're going to take this news, but I rather think you might have twins on the way!"

Tears began trickling down Charlie's face, which she tried bravely to wipe away with a handkerchief, but all to no avail, and now she was sobbing uncontrollably.

It was only two days after the depressing news that she wouldn't be able to stay with Corinne after she'd given birth. As her sobs began abating, she tearfully explained how all her plans had now come to nothing and she didn't know what on earth she was going to do. The doctor looked at Charlie with sympathetic eyes and inwardly felt deeply for her.

"I would strongly advise you to go home to your family, but if that's something you really feel unable to do, then our practice does have access to Beechwood Lodge, a church charity run hostel for single mums and their children. You'd give birth there and be able to stay for up to a month after which you would be advised to give up your babies for adoption if you had no practical way of supporting yourself. I know this all too much to take in now, so come back and see me in a week, but in the meantime, I'll reserve you a place at Beechwood because they're always in rather short supply," she said, observing the perplexed and confused look on Charlie's tear-stained face.

Chapter 13

Freelance feature writer Dan Smith enjoyed thoroughly researching an intended subject as much as he enjoyed the actual writing because it often gave him small insights which he could weave into the narrative to make the piece more interesting. A woman colleague had recently visited The Old Mill House on a touring holiday of North Devon and had happened to mentioned it as a possibility for his on-going Hidden Holiday Gems series. Dan, who lived and worked from a small apartment in Reading, had gone into research mode re the quiet village of Little Oreford and had turned up some quite interesting background information including the mill's surprising former use for highly illegal cannabis growing, cunningly hidden in plain sight, until a serious fire had exposed the operation. Even more interesting was the fact that its two Eastern European operatives had later been stabbed to death while working on a nearby farm. This was clearly not the sort of stuff that could be worked into his Hidden Gems series but might well be of interest at some future time. Spurred on by a reporter's instinct, he decided on impulse to call The Old Mill House and see if he could fix an interview appointment for say 11am the following morning, which happened to be a Tuesday, and if that worked out, then he'd leave home at 6am and could easily be in Little Oreford in time because the journey would be all motorways and dual carriageways right up until the last twenty miles. As it happened, it did work out, as impulsive actions often do, and Mill manager Ben Jameson was happy to see him.

Dan packed and overnight bag, just in case he decided to stay down there and look around for a couple of days. He'd noted that The Oreford Inn had accommodation but if that was full there'd bound to be somewhere else locally that he could stay.

It was also around 11am that Tuesday morning when Charlie emerged onto the lane outside the inn only to find her unsuspecting granddaughter suddenly at her side. "I've just finished my shift and my aunt tells me you want to look around the mill so shall I walk across with you and introduce you to my dad who runs the craft centre?"

Operation 'keep an eye on Mrs Andrews' had swung seamlessly into action. "So where does your aunt Corinne live my dear?" she asked, slipping her arm though Lottie's as they set off across the green. It seemed to be the most natural action in the world and she drew great comfort from it in the midst of her still emotional confusion as to whether she should tell them all the truth or be chauffeur driven out of their lives knowing that all was well in their world. "Oh, Auntie Corinne has a flat in the hotel which she moved into after coming to work in Yardley Upton and then amazingly discovering that mum was her twin sister." "Goodness me, you must tell me how that happened before I go, if there's time."

After the shock arrival of the letter from the council, Corinne and Charlie waited for their visitation from the housing officer. Charlie had planned to move back to her flat share after the funeral but her friend clearly didn't want her to go so, she'd stayed on 'just for a few days' which then extended into weeks.

The knock on the door finally came the day after Charlie was admitted to Beechwood because it had been decided that, as she was having twins, it would be better to have her in early to keep an eye on her.

Her baby girls were born late on a wet and windy June afternoon. It had been a reasonably easy and straightforward delivery with the first, whom she named Corinne after her dear friend, weighing into the world at just under six pounds, while her twin, who'd yet to be given a name, was just a little over five pounds. Both babies, having been given to Charlie for a few precious moments, were then taken off to the general nursery which would be their home for the next three to four weeks after which most of the infants would be offered up for adoption. For all had single mothers, mostly estranged from their families and with no means of support.

Charlie now found herself sleeping in a room with three other young mums, all with working class backgrounds and generally depressed with their circumstances. There was a communal dining room linked by a hatch to a large kitchen where, apart from looking after their babies and helping with the housework, the mums also had to help prepare, cook and serve their own meals.

Charlie had been so preoccupied with all that had been going on in her life, that she'd given little thought as to how she would feel about her babies when they arrived. She'd rather suspected that, like her own mother, she was not a person with strong maternal instincts.

But the moment she'd first held her precious pair all that changed and the very idea of giving them up was now totally abhorrent to her. Those around her all appeared to be either resigned to the adoption process, or so worn down by their circumstances that giving up their babies would actually be a relief. The fact that they appeared to have few, if any, visitors only served to emphasise their isolation. But there was no way Charlie was giving up her two, even if it meant walking out of Beechwood without telling anyone.

A possible way out of her dilemma manifested itself two afternoons after the twins were born with the arrival of Corinne and her next-door neighbour and close friend Joan, whom Charlie had got to know, and who'd attended George's funeral and travelled with them in the undertaker's chauffeur-driven car to the reception at The Star. They came with flowers, meeting Charlie in Beechwood's communal lounge, unusually empty at the time, and after they'd chatted for a few minutes, she went off to the nursery to return with Corinne, wrapped in a blanket, and sat down next to her elderly friend and surrogate mum.

"Corinne, meet baby Corinne. I'm naming her after you because of all the endless kindnesses you and dear George have shown me," she explained. "You didn't have to do that, my love, but I'm deeply honoured and I know my darling George would be too," she said leaning over and gently touching one of the child's tightly clenched hands. "Her sister, Laura's asleep so I've left her in her cot," she told them. "Oh, Laura's a nice name too, so is it after someone you know dear?" asked Corinne.

Charlie explained that she'd worked with a really nice girl, called Laura, at the events company and had also had a school friend called Laura.

"So, is there any news from the Council yet about the house, Corinne?" Charlie asked. "Yes, there is dear and it looks as if things might work out all right. They're offering me a one-bedroom flat in a small block just around the corner, but that's not the best news, is it Joan?" Charlie looked at them both, wondering just what might be coming next. "Well, it's like this. I'm going to have a spare bedroom shortly because my son is going off to spend a year with his dad, whose living in Australia these days, so why don't you move in on a temporary basis, just until you get yourself fixed up? There'd be enough room for a cot and Corinne can come around and help."

Charlie looked at their eager faces. "Oh, thank you so much. You don't know what a relief this is for me, but I will do my utmost to make sure that I don't impose on you for a minute longer than absolutely necessary," said Charlie. It was the following afternoon that she received a visit from Janice Monkton, the senior member of a small team of council sponsored health visitor come social workers attached to Beechwood and was interviewed in a small private office set aside for the purpose.

The middle-aged woman exuded a persona of sympathetic understanding while at the same time being totally realistic as to the practical possibilities facing Beechwood's mostly vulnerable young women because her chief responsibility was for the wellbeing of their new born babies.

It didn't take her many moments to realise that in Charlie Potter she was dealing with an intelligent and resourceful young woman, who just happened to have found herself in a vulnerable position. Charlie quickly found herself warming to her questioner and outlined her plan for moving in with Joan, who'd be there to support her with Corinne's willing assistance and how there was now the very real prospect of a job at the city's prestigious Star Hotel as soon as her babies were old enough to be left with her two friends.

"I'm relieved to hear that you have a clear plan for what happens when you leave Beechwood, but might I ask you just to consider the possibility of giving up one of your twins for adoption. I have a young couple in mind who have an excellent background and are quite desperate to give a good home to a child because they can't have one of their own. I don't need to tell you just how demanding it's going to be caring for one child without a husband at your side let alone twins." Charlie promised not to dismiss the suggestion out of hand and to give it some serious thought before Janice Monkton came again. She'd actually decided there and then that giving up one of her twins was the last thing she was going to do.

But as the days progressed and all the difficulties of looking after two infants rather than one became abundantly clear, she began having second thoughts. Would it be such a bad thing to allow a childless couple to lavish more care and attention on one of her cherished babies than she would ever be able to do? Besides that, it would mean that her remaining child would benefit from receiving all her attention instead of half of it.

Yes, however hard parting with one of her babies was going to be, it would be a selfless act which would bring a lot of joy and happiness into this childless couple's world, she eventually decided. Despite her resolution, the day she let Laura go was a terrible one and she wept for hours, all the heartache and worries of the past nine months bubbling to the surface in an outpouring of grief and past despairs. In the pre-dawn light of the following morning, she bitterly regretted her decision, but it was too late because her baby had already been taken away.

Chapter 14

Dan Smith left home early and stopped for breakfast at services just off the M5 close to its junction with the main access route to Tiverton and beyond into the heart of North Devon. It was now around 8.30am and he had plenty of time to be in Little Oreford just before 11am, He'd bought his smart roof garden apartment in a converted warehouse with the proceeds from the sale of his widowed mother's 1930s house in the town. It was her death that had brought him home from East Africa where he was the Communications Officer for a major international charity with extensive operations in the region. He could have moved back into his family home, but it held too many memories and it would sort have been going back rather than moving on. He'd fully intended returning to Africa but coming back home to Reading had unsettled him and he decided that perhaps it was time for a complete change of direction. So, when a close friend from his early daily newspaper days offered him regular freelance feature writing work on a weekend supplement for one of the nationals, he resigned from the charity.The great thing about being a freelance was that it allowed him to get out and about around the country and to simply take off on a whim if he could justify it and the visit to Little Oreford could certainly be justified in pursuit of another hidden gem. This quaint North Devon village on a plateau in the rolling landscape with several thatched cottages and a cluster of small houses around an open green, could certainly qualify as a hidden gem, he thought approvingly as he stepped out of his car and looked about him.

Glancing at his watch he saw he had twenty minutes to spare before his interview so decided on a stroll across the green.

Coming towards him was a young woman with an elderly lady on her arm. They paused and moved off to the right where there was a wooden seat.

"Are you sure you don't mind sitting with me for a few minutes before we go into the mill, Lottie?" asked Charlie. "Of course not, Mrs Andrews. That would be fine by me." Lottie had also become a little intrigued by their elderly and obviously quite wealthy guest because, after all, she was the first to have arrived in a chauffeur-driven limousine with a lady companion, but it was the young woman, who suddenly found herself in the spotlight.

"Now tell me all about yourself," Charlie said, turning and placing a soft hand on her unsuspecting granddaughter's wrist. "I'm not sure where I should begin," replied Lottie, feeling her face beginning to flush with embarrassment. She did not take after her more extrovert brother Luke, who'd always been the leader in all their games. "Well, are you on your summer break from college or university or do you have other career plans, my dear?"

"I'm in my final year of sixth form college and Mum and Dad would like me to go off to university, but, to tell you the truth, I'd far rather just stay around here and help my Auntie Corinne run The Oreford Inn and my parents with the mill and maybe do a little voluntary work. Dad says that if that's what I really want to do, then I should at least go and get a hotel and catering qualification and I guess I know he's right." She paused.

"There are also other reasons why I'd far rather stay around here." she admitted hesitantly.

"Ah, is one of them a boyfriend perhaps?" There was a hint of excitement in their elderly guest's voice and Lottie again felt her face colouring. "Yes, his name's Andy and he's our Commis Chef," she explained. "What do your parents and your Aunt Corinne think about that?" A look of embarrassment spread across her granddaughter's pretty face. "Is it that they don't know yet dear?" Lottie nodded. "He came just after Christmas and we've been hanging out together almost ever since."

"Why don't you just tell them dear? If he's a nice hard-working boy, which he obviously is since you've fallen for him, then why should they object? Lottie shook her head. "As he's my first boyfriend, I know they'd think it was just a crush and if they did object then Andy would feel he'd have to leave which I would hate and he'd hate too because he loves working here. So, we don't want to risk "

"Hmm, I see, dear. But how have you managed to keep it a secret, especially as you are always helping out?" she asked. "That's been pretty easy actually because he always has Mondays off and doesn't come in until noon on Tuesdays so I meet up with him on my college lunch breaks and free periods and sometimes I skive and we go off in his car for the day. When we're at work we do our best to ignore one another so it all works pretty well."

Charlie nodded knowingly. "Your secret's safe with me my dear. I guess you'll just have to work it out as time goes by because things often do work themselves out and sometimes in ways that you might not expect."

Lottie looked visibly relieved at having shared the secret that had been drilling a small hole in her conscience for months and before she knew it, she'd leant over and given Charlie a hug.

"Shall we go over to the mill now, or would you like to sit

here for a little longer," she asked, her mobile phone ringing in her pocket as she did so. It was her mum, Laura. "Where are you darling?" There was a detectable urgency in the question. "I'm sitting on the green with Mrs Andrews. Is there anything the matter?" she asked. "Yes. I've just done a big shop at the Allway Centre and now the car won't start and I'm told it will be at least ninety minutes before a recovery vehicle can reach me so can you pop over and pick up the shopping which needs to go in the freezer before it's ruined? I've already spoken to dad and he can't come because a journalist has arrived to do a feature about the mill." "OK, Mum, I'm on my way," she said before explaining the emergency to Charlie. "That's quite all right, dear. I'm enjoying sitting here in the sun so you can accompany me to the mill when you get back if you like."
Charlie watched her granddaughter hurry back across the green and disappear into the drive of Albany House only to emerge a couple of minutes later in a small car. Her instincts told her that before the end of the week she'd find a reason to visit her family home and come face to face with her other long lost, but never ever forgotten, daughter.

Chapter 15

It took weeks for Charlie to come to terms with giving away Laura, deeply regretting what she'd done, in the few quiet moments when she wasn't totally involved with looking after Corinne. She was turning out to be a particularly demanding baby, never wanting to be put down in her cot and then only sleeping for short periods. Her constant waking in the night and crying was also beginning to have its effect on her kind-hearted landlady Joan, who was beginning to wonder if taking in this lovely but homeless young mother had actually been a mistake. She'd had misgivings from the start but had been subtly persuaded by her life-long friend Corinne who had been through her own misery with the death of her beloved George.

Charlie could also sense things were not really working out and did her best to be out of the house as much as possible, spending long periods of time with Corinne in her tiny flat. She'd luckily managed to pick up an old but sturdy pram at the weekly bring and buy jumble sale and coffee mornings that she and her adopted mum attended in the nearby Methodist Church Hall. She'd also acquired a motley selection of well-worn and many times handed down baby clothes and some old plastic toys,

The sale and coffee mornings became something of a lifeline because they provided somewhere for Charlie and Corinne to go on Saturday mornings and it was not long before the mostly middle-aged and elderly regulars rallied round and began elping this lovely young woman who'd suddenly appeared in their midst.

After a few weeks, Charlie found herself helping out on one of the stalls with her battered old pram by her side and finding the pick of any suitable jumble items being hurriedly put on one side and reserved for her. The baby was a great attraction and it wasn't long before clothes were being knitted for her and she and Corinne were being invited out for afternoon teas. But while that was the bright spot in her now precarious existence, there were still many hours of walking the streets with her pram because she couldn't always be around at Corinne's and there was really nowhere else to go.

She was just managing on her meagre child allowance and was reluctantly receiving a little help from Corinne. Luckily as spring melted into summer, the weather became warm and sunny for quite long spells so she spent a lot of her time sitting on park benches and reading a whole variety of novels she'd picked up for nothing among all the practically unsellable items at the end of most sales.

Yes, those sunny days in the parks, the jumble sales and the help of all those lovely warm-hearted people, plus Corinne's constant support and encouragement, really were the bright spots in her largely itinerant existence all those years ago, Charlie mused, as she sat on the seat in the churchyard. But then it had all come to an abrupt end. For that July ushered in much cooler and damper weather as a series of lows crowded in from the North Atlantic. It was at the end of a particularly wet Monday afternoon that Charlie returned cold and miserable to her temporary home to find that Joan's routinely bad-tempered son Tom had returned early from Australia.

He'd fallen out with his father had now found his bedroom occupied and that he would be spending that night on the sofa in the lounge. It was an impossible situation,especially as Charlie quickly discovered he was not an understanding sort of person and she'd have to move out just as soon as she possibly could.

She spent a miserable night agonising for long hours on just what she should do next. Strangely, as if some instinct had come into play, her baby went down without any fuss and slept all night in her cot and had not had to be taken into her mother's single bed. Surely it was time to give up and go home and throw herself on the mercy of her parents who'd regard her single mum status as a disgrace that would have inevitably to be shared with their ever dwindling but God-fearing congregation. She'd either have to rely completely on their charity or find a job and leave Corinne in the care of her mother and sister and she had a pretty good idea how that would go down.

No, going home in disgrace was not an option. Maybe her old flatmate could help out for a few days, she wondered just before falling mercifully into an exhausted sleep. Kate had decided not to bother sharing anymore after Charlie had gone to live with Joan, because she didn't really need the money and flatmates were generally more trouble than they were worth and was now actually enjoying having the place to herself. Charlie called her from a phone box the following morning, managing to keep its heavy swing door open by leaning against it in order to watch her hooded pram parked out on the pavement in a steady drizzle. Just battling with the door seemed to emphasize how much she was being weighed down by her unhappy existence.

Kate wanted to say 'no' to helping her now desperate friend in her hour of need, but simply couldn't bring herself to do it and abandoned her research project to go and help. Joan, who was feeling guilty, even though she'd done her best, knew she had no choice other to reclaim the room for her son. She called a friendly local taxi man she'd used over the years and a few minutes after his arrival, he found himself dismantling the cot. The move was completed in a couple of round trips and by the end of the day Charlie and her baby, plus the cot and her few clothes and personal belongings were back in her old room in Clifton. "Realistically Charlie you really can't go on like this, especially as you're determined not to go back home," Kate said sympathetically after the baby had gone down and they were sitting together with two large glasses of red wine, having consumed large portions of hurriedly cooked pasta. "I know and I feel really awful inflicting myself on you again." There was a long silence as Kate considered whether, seeing her friend's distressed state, this was the time to say what was on her mind and then decided that it was. "If you're determined not to go home to North Devon, I really don't know what else you can do other than give Corinne up," she said quietly.

Yes, that really has been her lowest point, Charlie agreed with herself as her wandering thoughts brought her back from the past to her sunny seat on the village green. Just how could she have brought herself to giving

up Corinne rather than returning home to Albany House. she'd asked herself time and again over the years.
Yet miraculously all had worked out well in the end and just how had her girls found their way back to Little Oreford, she wondered for the umpteenth time? Might it be possible to find out, without their realising, she was their mother, or would she have to tell them the truth and admit to abandoning them rather than going home in disgrace. No. She'd still not decided what to do but perhaps the answer would come to her before they left on Sunday.

"You're still here then Mrs Andrews! so shall we go over to the mill now?" There was a surprised note in her granddaughter's voice. "Yes, I'm still here dear," replied Charlie, looking up and smiling. "But no. It must be almost lunchtime so perhaps I'll go this afternoon."

Chapter 16

Dan Smith found his interviewee, Ben Jameson, behind an oak reception desk flanked by leaflet stands displaying much of what there was to see and do around this corner of North Devon. "Let's go into my office for a coffee and a chat before I show you around," he invited after they exchanged greetings. "I can keep an eye on the desk through the glass door and pop out should anyone come but I don't expect we'll be disturbed." Dan said a black coffee with no sugar would be good and looked around at his surroundings as Ben filled two brightly-coloured mugs from a coffee pot on a hot plate. "These were made in our working pottery, which is one of our most popular attractions, and you'll find Shelley our potter a most interesting person to talk to. Archie, our resident wood turner and carver, also has quite a tale about how he came to be here, if that would be of interest to your readers," Ben explained. "Do tell me about the mill itself before we have a wander around," Dan invited. He wondered if the manager would mention the devastating fire that had broken out while the place was being used by a criminal gang for growing cannabis in plain sight, ten years earlier and how its two Polish growers, who'd escaped, had later been brutally murdered while working on a nearby farm. This wasn't the story he was going to write on this occasion because it had no relevance, but maybe later when the Hidden Gems series was done and dusted. He'd enjoyed doing the research which had brought the mill's troubled past to light and having 'one up' on this unsuspecting manager.

This was the more perverse and cynical side of his nature, but he kept it well hidden in the shadow of his outwardly sunny and mostly extrovert personality which encouraged the people he was interviewing to 'open up' to him.

Ben told how the flour mill had been built in the 14th century, powered by a stream that had long since ceased to flow, and how a substantial house had later been erected beside it. "All the mill's old machinery is surprisingly intact, as you'll see later, and we have a long-term project to replace the stream with a big generator and get it operational again." Dan made a quick note, because that was of interest, and asked just how long term that was. "It's the usual case of how long it's going to take us to raise £100,000. We've applications in for grants with all the usual suspects, including the National Lottery, but these things all take time and, in reality, we're never going to be a priority because getting an old mill working again isn't very sexy these days," he admitted.

"My colleague who stayed in Little Oreford a few weeks ago mentioned that you'd had a fire here some years ago," Dan said innocently. It was a lie, but it would be interesting to hear the response. "That's true and it was a blessing in disguise because we were able to buy the property, plus the mill, for a very affordable price from its owners who lived abroad and hadn't been near the place for years and had it rented out at the time." "Who was the 'we' if I might ask?" The matter-of-fact question sounded innocent enough, but suddenly put Ben on his guard, especially as he'd omitted mentioning the cannabis growing that had caused the fire in the first place.

"I'm not sure how this is relevant to your Hidden Gems feature but, for what it's worth, we have private investors who prefer to stay in the background." Sensing that he'd asked one question too many. Dan quickly returned to asking about the mill's activities. "I'll certainly make the mill a feature of my piece and I could even put your fundraising details in the Fact File which accompanies it," he offered. "That would be most appreciated, but what are you doing about lunch?" Ben asked as the tour around was coming to an end. He was now feeling more

at ease with their inquisitive visitor. "Lunch at our Oreford Inn is an essential part of our visitor experience so my sister-in-law Corinne has taken the liberty of reserving you a table as our guest if that would suit."
Dan said that it would suit very nicely and that he'd be delighted to accept their generous hospitality. This was all a most interesting family set-up he thought as he strolled across the green towards the inn and just who were these private investors? he wondered.

Corinne Potter was waiting to welcome him at the door, tipped off by a call from Ben, and showed him to one of the three best tables for two beside the mullioned windows overlooking the green. "He's pretty inquisitive so be a little careful about what you say to him, especially as he started asking me about the fire and who'd bought the mill afterwards. But he's going to give a good plug for the restoration project which might just give us the fundraising kick start we need."

Corinne surprised herself by finding her tall and slightly gangly guest with his still quiet boyish face and blond hair instantly attractive.

They shook hands and even that simple connection stirred something within her for his handshake was firm and had it been held it for fractionally longer than was polite? Corinne handed him a menu, saying she'd be back a little later when the lunchtime service was over and that perhaps she might join him for coffee to answer any questions he might have. Dan, who'd already noticed she wasn't wearing a wedding ring, looked up at her and smiled, saying he'd very much appreciate that. Maybe he should stick around for a couple of days, especially if there was room at the inn, because he quite fancied slightly older women, he thought as he watched her walk away.

Lost deep in her thoughts, Charlie remained sitting on the green. She'd avoided dwelling on her giving up of Corinne for many years and mercifully the passage of time had healed over the wound, but the flood gates were opening again and she knew there was no way of stemming all those painful memories. Now she was back on a particularly wet late November afternoon, pushing Corinne through Bristol's busy Broadmead shopping centre without a bean in her pocket and under subtle, but growing pressure from her flatmate Katie to find somewhere else to live. The widows were full of Christmas fare which only served to heighten her sense of loneliness and near despair.

A blast of warm air met her as she entered yet another department store on her aimless wander and bumped straight into Janice Monkton from Beechwood, her arms weighed down with Christmas shopping. One look at Charlie's unhappy face told the whole story and she insisted they go straight to the cafeteria for tea and cakes and a catch-up chat.

The place was packed but Janice soon found a table lost in the corner and insisted that Charlie sat down while she queued for tea and toasted teacakes. Trying hard to keep back the tears, she told Janice all that had happened since she'd left Beechwood. "You do know that you really can't go on like this," said Janice, her voice full of sympathy and as if, right on cue, baby Corinne stirred in her pram and began crying. So, she had given up her baby for adoption. But then she was recalling how, on a whim, she'd emptied out the contents of her red leather shoulder bag, scribbled a brief note on a scrap of paper and thrust it deep inside a pocket together with a treasured childhood photograph and had told Janice Monkton she wanted her child to have something to remember her by.

Charlie had taken up the kindly Star General Manager's invitation to go and work for him. It had not been an easy decision because of all the Brad memories, but in the end, she'd realised that she didn't really have an alternative. It had turned out to be the best move she'd ever made in her young and then greatly troubled life.

With her striking good looks and sunny outgoing personality, Charlie would be ideal for a front of house role, the manager decided, so she'd start learning the ropes on reception. At first, she found it slightly odd to be working alongside the much older woman professional she'd nodded to so many times when popping in to see dear George and for weeks she'd avoided going anywhere near the guest bedroom she'd shared with Brad.

But those feelings faded as she began working her way up through all the traditional hotel roles from reception and back office, through to housekeeping and finally to food and beverages. From there it was but as short step to Duty Manager and then finally to Deputy General Manager.

By that time, her kindly boss had retired to be replaced by a younger man who quickly came to appreciate her qualities and so helped to progress her career. Charlie visited Corinne, her adopted mum, at least once a week and every year on the anniversary of George's death they had a meal in The Star's restaurant. After four years and Corinne's sudden death from a stroke, she'd finally left to take up her first Acting General Manager's position with another of the hotel group's properties in Oxford.

There'd been relationships along the way but running an hotel was a demanding business and that always came first so they all came to nothing in the end, not that she was really that bothered. Hotel Group colleagues were now her extended family and she was largely content with that. A further six years and two hotels later, she took up the group's offer to go and assist in the opening of their first property in the Caribbean and that was where she met and fell in love with her beloved Hugo Andrews. He was a young, but sadly widowed property developer with a seven-year-old son who happened to hire the hotel's main conference suite to showcase a new villa style complex to potential investors.

The Church clock struck 1.45pm, pulling Charlie back from her memories.

'Oh dear, if I don't get back, I'll miss lunch,' she thought, getting to her feet and heading for the inn at a little faster than her normal pace. She could certainly move if she wanted to because several years of daily walks along the Sidmouth promenade with Annie had helped to keep her in trim. Thankfully there were still a few other diners in the restaurant, but she was slightly annoyed on seeing that he was favourite window seat was occupied by a young man and that her daughter had just gone over to join him. "I think you have another late diner," said Dan, who'd spotted her hovering in the restaurant doorway. Corinne turned to see Mrs Andrews. "Excuse me a moment. I'll just go and find her a table. "Have you had a nice morning," she asked brightly, showing Charlie to the window. seat, two tables beyond where the journalist was seated. "Yes, I sat on the green and had a lovely chat with your niece, Lottie, but I never made it over to the mill, so hopefully I will manage it this afternoon." Corinne pulled back the chair facing away from her journalist guest, but Charlie chose the one opposite, saying she always preferred to look into a room rather than out of it.

"That was an excellent lunch," Dan declared as Corinne sat down and asked if he'd care for another coffee, an offer which he willingly accepted as a means of settling in for a good chat with this most attractive woman. He started telling her about the Hidden Gems series which had given him a wonderful opportunity to travel around the country staying in some really lovely out of the way places, all on expenses of course

"There's only one flaw that I can see which is that once you've thrown the spotlight on these places in the national press, then they're not going to be hidden gems anymore," Corinne challenged. "That's true but why shouldn't people be encouraged to get out into the countryside and help boost the economy of rural areas that could often do with the investment?" he responded. "I'm sure your brother-in-law Ben would be delighted if my piece brings lots more people to the mill and then to stay on or have a meal in this lovely old coaching inn and talking of which might you have a room available this evening?" The suddenness of the request, took Corinne by surprise. "Yes. I think we do, but I'll have to check just in case something's come in this morning while I've been out."

Corinne experienced a slight tingle of excitement as she walked back to reception because it had been ages since she'd felt an attraction for a man. True, she'd got to know several unattached businessmen, who'd stayed on a regular basis in recent years, but she'd never really taken much notice of them because, for a start, they'd shown no interest in the inn, but somehow this was different. 'Calm down. You're a forty three-year old woman and not a young girl with a crush,' she told herself. She returned to the table with the good news that there was a room but only for one night. However, if he wanted to stay longer, a new bed and breakfast had opened next to the Red Lion just down the road in Hampton Green. "So, how did you come to be manager here," he asked after giving her a brief outline of his more recent past.

Two tables away, Charlie had overheard almost every word with mounting excitement at the sudden prospect of learning something of her daughter's past life!

"That's rather a long story and I certainly don't have the time to go into it right now." It was the perfect opening, thought Dan. "So how about supper this evening?" The suddenness of the suggestion caught Corinne completely off her guard and just for a moment she felt flustered.

"It couldn't be here because we're quite busy this evening and although I'm not on duty, I'd find myself being distracted, keeping an eye on things." The real reason was that if, and it was a big if, this was going any further, then she certainly didn't want the whole village knowing about it from the very outset. "How about the Red Lion in Hampton Green, if they do food?" he suggested. "They do but it's quiz night and the place will be packed, but there is Frankie's Italian Bistro in Draymarket which is only a short drive from here." With that, Dan took out his mobile, quickly found and called the bistro and booked a table for two for eight o'clock. "That's settled then, so what time should we leave?" he asked smiling. "You certainly don't waste any time do you," she replied, returning his smile. "There's no time like the present, I say."

So, Corinne was going out on a date which was exciting, but she'd now have to find another way of learning all about her daughter's past, thought Charlie. Then Brad's face appeared and, in an instant, she'd caught a sense of the excitement she herself had felt all those years ago.

Chapter 17

Annie and Bob drove most of the way home in a companionable silence, each lost in their own thoughts. Annie could not remember a day she'd enjoyed quite so much and was now feeling excited over all that might lie ahead. There had been no word from the Oreford Inn so they could assume that Charlie had not gone on too much of a walkabout and they'd be back in an hour. Bob's thoughts had lingered on the bikers and how their road trip had suddenly been ruined. He'd given them his card. but he doubted he'd ever hear from them again. Then his thoughts turned to tonight's quiz at the Red Lion. "Annie, I don't suppose you could join Hannah, Heather and I for the pub quiz tonight?" he asked. "Oh! That would be lovely, but I really don't think I should disappear for a second night running."

It was late afternoon by the time Bob dropped her off outside the inn. "If you should change your mind about tonight just call and I'll come and pick you up," he said. Annie found Charlie sitting in the small lounge. "Oh! there you are, dear. I've had a lovely afternoon looking around the old mill with Ben. He really is such a nice man. Have you had a nice day?" Annie sat down beside Charlie and told her all about their trip. "I think you might be getting quite sweet on him," she said, suddenly, fixing her with a questioning look. Annie experienced a ridiculous feeling of embarrassment welling up inside her. It was as if she was a young girl being quizzed about her first date, which was ridiculous. "Yes, you are. I can see it written all over your face," she pressed. Denials were now pointless.

"OK, yes. We had such a lovely day and to tell you the truth I hadn't felt so happy for a long time," she confessed. "I'm so pleased for you! So, what's Bob doing tonight?" Annie was being cornered and she knew it so how should she respond? She really would like to join Bob for the quiz, but should she? After all she'd been out all day and wouldn't she be failing in her duty to go off yet again? "Bob's going to a quiz with the two ladies who run the B&B where he's staying, but he has offered to come and pick me up," she admitted. "That's settled then. You must go, so give him a call right now," she pressed. "But what about you?" Annie asked, still feeling a twinge of guilt. "I shall be fine with a little supper in my room because I've had a lovely day and I'm actually feeling quite tired now."

Charlie stood in her bedroom window, overlooking the green and just above The Oreford Inn sign and watched as Bob's Bentley pulled up outside and moved off again a few moments later. She was really enjoying encouraging this little romance and was looking forward to doing all she could to make it flourish, but now her thoughts were turning back to the events of that momentous afternoon. It had given her such a secret thrill to be shown around and treated like a VIP by her completely unsuspecting son-in-law. They'd sat down together in the mill's small tea room after her tour and he'd asked if there was anything else that he could show her. Corinne had asked him to keep an eye on this special guest and to his surprise, what he'd thought was going to be a chore, had turned out to be a real pleasure. She had been so friendly and attentive, even placing her arm unexpectedly though his as if she was some favourite nephew.

"There is one small favour I would like to ask," she replied. "And what might that be Mrs Andrews?" She paused. "Do you think it might be possible for you or your wife to dhow me around your lovely old house which looks so inviting standing there at the end of your lawn?" The sudden request was the last thing Ben had expected. "Why don't you come in for a cuppa say around 4pm tomorrow because I'm sure Laura would be delighted to show you around, although I'd better check first that she's not got anything on," he'd replied. A message had come back later saying her daughter was free and would be delighted to meet her. Just then there was a quiet tap on the door announcing the arrival of her supper. It had been prepared in the kitchen below by the Oreford Inn's' Commis Chef Andy Taylor, whose mind had definitely not been on his work because he was mentally making plans for the following day which he would be spending with Lottie at the beginning of a week's holiday. She'd told her parents that after college, she was going on to a party with her two best girlfriends after which they'd be having a sleepover. Ben and Laura trusted their daughter implicitly because having sleepovers had become part of her life ever since she'd turned eighteen, some six months earlier, and all had been fine. They knew her friend's parents and had made discrete check calls on the first couple of occasions to find that all was as it should be, but tomorrow night there was to be no sleepover. Instead, Andy and Lottie planned to spend the day and the night together. They'd already started love making in a variety of not particularly comfortable places because the bedsit he shared with two untidy friends was a tip and he'd always resisted taking her there.

But tomorrow would be different because they'd be spending the night at his aunt's summerhouse near the

North Devon coast. It was normally let out at this time of the year, but this particular week it happened to be free and his aunt had happily agreed he could use it. They'd both be driving in their own cars so that Lottie could be back home after college the following late afternoon, although she'd no intention of going to college.

Charlie had just settled herself in the armchair beside the now slightly open window with her supper tray in front of her when Dan Smith's smart two-seater sports car pulled up outside the Oreford Inn and Corinne Potter emerged and got into it. But their evening at Frankie's Italian Bistro in Draymarket was not destined to be a success. Her initial attraction to the Hidden Gems journalist wore off as the evening wore on. There was only one other couple having supper in the bistro which, unknown to her, had recently changed hands and now lacked the charm of its former genial host. Dan, she quickly came to realise, was rather self-opinionated and gently and quite persuasively over inquisitive about what made Little Oreford tick, so the more he pried, the more defensive she became. He clearly knew something about the fire at The Old Mill a decade ago and probably about all that had followed after that, although he had not said so. It suddenly occurred to her, probably quite irrationally, that the tenth anniversary of the blaze, that had affected so many lives, was actually the following month and that maybe this journalist who had suddenly appeared on the scene was more interested in that then writing his Hidden Gems feature.

Dan also quickly sensed their evening was not going quite as he'd planned it, so it was just before 10pm when they got back to the Inn and bid each other good night. Corinne was now highly relieved they had no vacancy the following evening and was hoping this journalist would call it a day and not take up her earlier, and with hindsight foolish, suggestion, that he could book into the B&B next to The Red Lion in Hampton Green. She made sure she was not around when he had breakfast and checked out the following morning and hoped that was the last they'd be seeing of him. Dan had fully intended staying at the B&B, but when he got back to his room and checked his messages, there was one from his editor asking him to return to London because 'something had come up.

While the evening was dragging on in Frankie's Italian Bistro, the pub quiz at the Red Lion was in full throttle. It was not known for being an orderly affair, but tonight it was particularly raucous and Annie and Bob, Hannah and Heather were right in the middle of it. "Is it always like this?" Annie asked shouting to make herself heard, during one particularly noisy moment when the quiz master, a rotund, jolly faced and extremely quick-witted retired teacher, was remonstrating with a woman on the next table for challenging his answer to one of the questions. "Oh, yes, those two are always having a go at one another and that's all part of the fun," replied Heather. Bob was sitting in front of his second empty glass of zero alcohol beer, having downed a pint of the real locally brewed stuff much earlier and was wondering whether he should risk just another half of the local brew before driving Annie back to Little Oreford.

They'd all been having such a laugh and he couldn't remember when he'd enjoyed himself quite so much. Annie caught his eye. She was smiling and it seemed to him she was saying, they now shared something special. "Look you two. It would be a pity to break up the party when we're all having such a great time. So do you really have to go back to Little Oreford tonight when we have an empty guest room for you Annie?" Heather suddenly suggested. "Yes, oh do stay," joined in Hannah. Bob and Annie glanced at one another as the unspoken possibility of what that could mean dawned on both of them. "Look don't worry about the old girl, she'll be fast asleep by now and from what you've told us about her, she won't mind in the slightest," pressed

Hannah. "Well, OK, but I'll go outside and give The Oreford Inn a call so they will know how to get hold of us if there were a problem," said Annie, getting to her feet and weaving her way through the packed tables to reach the door.

It was if the brakes had suddenly been taken off and they'd all had far more than a drop to drink by the time they linked arms to steady themselves and had walked the few hundred yards back to the barn for a final round of nightcaps. Heather showed Annie into the second guest bedroom and produced a night shirt and some extra toiletries to compliment the guest ones in the ensuite and closed the door behind her. So, what now? But before she'd gathered her thoughts, she heard a gentle tap on the door; it was Bob. "We didn't really say goodnight," he said, standing hesitantly in the doorway. "No, we didn't replied Annie, drawing him slowly and unresisting into the room and wrapping her arms around him for a lingering kiss.

"I think we'd better close the door now, don't you?" she said, releasing him from her arms. They began undressing one another between kisses that quickly became more and more frantic as if after many months of celibacy there was simply no time to lose. He couldn't wait to enter her and she was now mentally crying out to receive him. Afterwards they lay wrapped in one another's arms before quickly falling asleep.

Chapter 18

Bob drove Annie back to Little Oreford early the following morning. They spoke little on the journey with Annie expressing how she felt by gently caressing the back of his neck. They parted, exchanging quick kisses and agreeing he should return to the barn for his breakfast and to await further instructions. So, what would today hold she wondered as she made her way quietly up the stairs and back into her room for a quick shower and a change of clothes.

Just a few feet away on the other side of a centuries old lathe and plaster wall, Charlie was lying wide awake, despite an unsettled night agonising over whether or not to reveal her other identity as the mother who'd given her twin baby daughters up for adoption. If she was going to do so, then time was running out because it was now Thursday morning and they were supposed to be leaving on Saturday. Perhaps the opportunity would come when she was being shown around dear old Albany House that afternoon, but if not then, it would have to wait to some future time, maybe a return visit in the autumn. Yes, that was it. She would arrange to come back for another holiday in October. There was a quiet tap and Annie popped her head around her door to see if she was awake. "Come in, come in. I want to hear all about your evening. Come and sit on the side of my bed." Annie did as she was told, now wondering just how much she should tell Charlie, but having the feeling that it really would be pointless, if not a little deceitful, to make out she'd come back to the inn last night if the question was asked and not simply assumed.

Anyway, she had the uncomfortable feeling that Miss Charlotte would have the whole story out of her come what may and she was not to be disappointed. "I'm so pleased for you dear. I've been thinking for months that a lovely young girl like you should not be on your own and now you're not and if I hadn't decided on having this lovely little holiday you and Bob would never have got together," she said, a small note of triumph in her voice. "So where is he now?" she asked. "He's back at the B&B having breakfast and waiting for you to decide if you would like to go out for another drive around today," Annie replied. "Oh no. My plans are already made because Ben's invited me to go and meet his wife, Laura, and to have a look around Albany House this afternoon." She paused. "Well actually that's not quite true because I invited myself and they happily accepted my invitation. So, you must call Bob to come and collect you and then you could go off to the North Devon coast for the day. I haven't been that way since I was a girl, but I seem to remember it's quite beautiful with some lovely cliffs and wooded bays, particularly around Lynmouth. "How could a girl refuse an invitation like that," laughed Annie, throwing up her arms in mock surrender. "And it's such a lovely day too!"

Bob took no persuading and just over an hour later, they were heading for the coast with Annie looking down at a map she'd borrowed from Corinne. "Remember when we were around at Royston and Alicia's the other night, she suggested Lynmouth and the Doone Valley as a place we could take Charlie if she wanted a longer day out. Apparently, she and Royston first started going there before they were married and now have a holiday place just along the coast. The only thing is, the way to it looks to be along a lot of minor roads which might not be suitable for us," she pointed out. "Don't worry because I'm well up for a challenge," laughed Bob.

Charlie watched them go from her bedroom window eyrie and now took herself down to the dining room for a late breakfast and hopefully to have another chat with daughter. She was in luck because Corinne, who'd been keeping her head down doing some paperwork in her office until she was sure Dan was safely on his way, now emerged just as Charlie was coming down. "Good morning, Mrs Andrews. How are you this morning?" But the reply was not quite what she was expecting! "I'm feeling footloose and fancy free now that I've sent my minders off for the day!" She replied with a twinkle in her eye. Corinne smiled. She was really going to miss this enigmatic older guest when she left on Saturday. She could not shake off the unerring feeling there was something more to her arrival in their midst in a chauffeur-driven Bentley with a woman companion, than just to have a 'little holiday. But what that was, she had no idea. "I hear you are going to have tea with my sister Laura this afternoon, so what are your plans for this morning?" she inquired, showing Charlie to her favourite table beside the window overlooking the green. "I'm going to visit your lovely old church and then find some shady seat to rest a while before lunch, but do tell me, who lives in that lovely old chocolate box cottage opposite?" she asked casually.

"Oh, that's Robin and his sister, Margo Lloyd. They've been here much longer than all of us, but they're away on a world cruise at the moment and won't be back for another week. Charlie turned her head towards the window, as if now peering across at the cottage, in a desperate attempt to avoid her daughter seeing the tears that had suddenly welled up and were now trickling uncontrollably down her face. She faked a cough and asked Corinne if she could kindly fetch her a glass of water, in a further attempt to hide her tears. Luckily, her daughter was waylaid by another guest and by the time she returned, Charlie had mopped away her tears in one of the linen table napkins. She managed to compose herself enough to ask Corinne for a poached egg on a slice of brown toast and to avoid the little chat to which she had so been looking forward.

Sitting in the pew she and her mother and sister Cynthia always occupied while listening dutifully to her father's sermons on those Sunday mornings so long ago, Charlie slowly came to terms with the shock news that her best friends Robin and Margo were still living in the village. They never went to church because neither of their parents 'believed in it' and it wasn't long before Charlie also came to the conclusion that she didn't 'believe in it' either and that she'd far rather be out with them than stuck in this depressing old place being forced to listen to her father's boring old sermons which seemed to drag on and on. But her confrontational childhood and her animosity towards her parents, out of whose lives she'd stormed so long ago, had tempered over the years. She'd reached a point where she tried only to remember the happier times and there had been a few of those, including the surprisingly proud look on her father's face the day he heard just how well she had done in her A Levels, despite never seeming to do any revision. Administering to his slowly dwindling flock and officiating at far more funerals than baptisms or weddings had been his life's work, supported unquestioningly by her mother and there was nobleness of spirit in devoting their lives to the service of others which she certainly had not appreciated in her younger days.

She was pondering on this while wandering slowly around the churchyard looking for their graves, which she knew must surely be there, among all the other ageing and weathered headstone, because where else could they possibly be? Then she spotted the name 'Potter' standing out in black lettering on a substantial white marble memorial near an ancient yew tree on the edge of the churchyard but it was not her father or mother's name, but that of Cynthia her older sister! She, it was now revealed, had died some years earlier than her parents, whose names followed, having been interred in the same family plot. Her father, it appeared had died in his 84th year, but her mother had lived on to be ninety-seven before joining him. So, what had become of Cynthia. Had she never left home or had she made her own way in the world before coming back to

Little Oreford? Charlie wondered, now feeling a rising sense of regret that she'd never returned or even attempted to make contact with them.

So if Robin and Margo had been living in Little Oreford for a long time, they'd surely be able to tell her something more about her family. But that would have to wait until she returned to the village in early October.

As it was a little too early for lunch, she'd go and while away a pleasant hour on that seat where she'd had such a nice chat with her granddaughter Lottie, but, oh dear, it was occupied by two gents with rucksacks beside them and flask cups in their hands.

"Good morning. Are you gentlemen of the road?" she enquired, immediately engaging them in conversation. "No, not exactly, but we are following a long-distance path called the Two Moors Way between Dartmoor and Exmoor and we've discovered that churchyard seats make excellent coffee stops and should it be raining, then there's usually a stone bench in the church porch in which to shelter," the slightly older one told her. "What a wonderful way to spend your days! So have you done many long walks?" "We've actually walked across England four times now, over the past thirty years," his companion explained. Now Charlie was in her most animated element and kept them talking until she'd learned how their names were Nigel and Peter and that they'd both met while working on newspapers in the West Country as young journalists and were still involved with the media after all these years. "So where are you going now?"

They were heading for Barnstable and would then be making their way along the North Devon coast to journeys end in Lynmouth, they told her. "Well, I wish you both all the best," said Charlie who'd now spotted another shady seat under a giant beech tree close by. But as she turned to leave a thought struck her. "How might I get in touch with you because I might have a story to tell one day?" she said. "I can help there," said Nigel, opening his plastic map case and producing a card which she took and slipped into her pocket. Settled on her seat, she watched as they gave her a friendly wave and then followed their progress along the church path until they were out of sigh.

Charlie had a bar snack for lunch and retired to her room for a rest until it was time to visit Albany House. She couldn't help returning again to the events of that unhappy afternoon at Beechwood so long ago when she'd cradled her infant Laura in her arms one last time before giving her up for adoption.

Now she was walking slowly up the drive towards Albany House. It felt as if she was at last going home after a life time. She could feel tears welling up, but somehow managed to keep her emotions under control. No, meeting Laura with tears rolling down her cheeks would definitely not be a good idea,"How lovely to meet you Mrs Edwards." Laura must have been keeping an eye open and was now coming towards her. Charlie stopped, her heart missing a beat. Her twins were identical, a possibility she'd never even considered. "Mrs Andrews! It's a pleasure to welcome you to our home, especially as I've heard so much about you from Ben and Corinne. But I'm not sure Albany House is of any particular architectural merit though, unless you know something we don't." said Laura. For a split second, Charlie was tempted to say: 'I may be Mrs Andrews now but I was once Charlotte Potter.

'I am your mother and this was my childhood home!' Instead, she smiled, saying she knew little about property and even less about old houses. "My only reason for wanting to call was to make your acquaintance. I've so enjoyed meeting Corinne, who could not have made me more welcome at the inn and then I had a lovely long chat with your daughter Lottie on the seat on the green before meeting Ben. So, I really felt something would have been missing had I not met you before we leave on Saturday." "I'm flattered so do come in," said Laura leading Charlie into the tiled hallway with the its lovely old oak staircase, she recognised instantly, and then on into the drawing room with its high ceiling and tiled open fireplace.

Again, all was almost as she remembered it from her childhood.

"What a lovely room," said Charlie, looking about her after settling herself in a comfortable, winged armchair in front of which, tea for two had been laid out on a coffee table "It looks to me as if it has been lovingly furnished to suit its period surroundings and it would not surprise me if the whole house was the same," she added. "How perceptive you are," said a delighted Laura, going on to tell Charlie all about the restoration programme they'd carried out after moving into Albany House some ten years earlier and how her neighbours, and by then the kids' adopted uncle and aunt Margo and Robin Lloyd had helped! For the second time that afternoon, Charlie was overcome with emotion on learning, right out of the blue, that her childhood friends were now regarded as proxy members of the family by her own daughter and son-in-law and her two grandchildren.

Again, she struggled to maintain her composure. An overwhelming rush of other memories surfaced as she followed Laura, first into what they called their Garden Room, overlooking the patio and rear lawn, and then into the big kitchen where she immediately saw that a modern Aga had replaced the one she remembered. Then they were climbing those stairs she'd climbed so many times before, all too often in a rush as she was being sent to her room and told not to come down until supper time. The second stair from the landing was still squeaking as it had done in her day. It made her feel instantly at home. All too soon the visit was over and she was walking slowly back to the inn, now in a complete turmoil over whether to reveal her true identity before she went home on Saturday.

Perhaps she should invite Ben and Laura over to the inn for supper with Corinne before she left as a thank-you and then break the news. Yes, that might be a plan, but the more she turned it over in her mind, the more she realised that when it actually came to it, she would most likely keep her secret because, for some inexplicable reason, something was holding her back. But then another thought struck her because having rediscovered her family, she wasn't at all sure she wanted to go on residing at Ocean View any more. Yes, she would go

back in Saturday, but when she returned in October, she'd find a house to purchase in the neighbourhood. Then a far more exciting thought struck her. Why wait until then when she had a chauffeur and a lovely companion to take her house hunting tomorrow!
And hadn't Annie and Bob been to a barbecue hosted by the area's leading estate agent only a couple of evenings ago!

The two were driving slowly back towards Little Oreford having enjoyed the happiest of days out together when his hands-free phone burst into life and Corinne Potter's voice filled the space. Annie's heart sank. The Oreford's manager was unlikely to be calling unless there was some emergency involving Miss Charlotte. "Hi. I'm calling because Mrs Andrews would like you both to join her in the residents' lounge when you get back because she wants to discuss some plans for tomorrow." Bob said they'd be back shortly. "I wonder what the old girl's cooking up this time Annie," he laughed. "I don't mind because whatever it is, it's obviously going to be involving the two of us and that's all right by me," she said.

They sensed immediately that Charlie was in a state of high excitement when they joined her in the lounge, leaving them both wondering what on earth was coming next. "Now do tell me all about your day before we talk about tomorrow," she invited when they were settled with a large pot of tea and a plate of shortbread biscuits in front of them. Annie told how they'd decided not to drive down the lanes to the Doone Valley, as suggested by Alicia Randall, because they were not really suitable for the Bentley, but had gone straight to Lynmouth and had walked up the River Lyn to Watersmeet for lunch before strolling back again. "The path wound its way up a beautiful wooded valley with the water rushing beside it which was an absolute delight, wasn't it Bob? But now you must tell us what you have in mind for tomorrow." Charlie took a deep breath as if needing it to encompass the enormity of her plan.

"I've decided I like Little Oreford and all the kind people we've met here so much that I'm going to come and live hereabouts, so tomorrow we're all going house hunting. I shall be looking for a substantial property so that I can employ a live-in companion and a chauffeur in their own separate accommodation and if you and Bob wish to apply then you'll be engaged immediately. So, what do you both think of that?" Bob hesitated. "Surprise is the only word which springs to mind, but also honoured you should think so highly of us," said Bob looking at Annie for confirmation."It is lovely around here, she agreed, but it's going to take some thinking about," said Annie guardedly. "And besides that, a substantial property hereabouts is going to cost a small fortune," she pointed out. "That's all right then because I have a large fortune at my disposal so we can all go house hunting tomorrow," said Charlie with that unmistakable twinkle in her eyes. "Oh, and one other thing, I want to stay on here for another week if there's room and of course, you are both willing to stay if you wish."

Charlie had earlier come to the conclusion that if Robin and Margo were returning in a few days, as Laura had told her, then there was no way she'd wait until October before being reunited with them again. Bob said he had another job on the following Tuesday so that wasn't going to be possible, but he'd certainly be free to come back and collect her and Annie the following Saturday if that was how things worked out. Annie said she'd have to check if Sam and Sally Owen would be happy for her to stay on or whether they needed her back at Ocean View.

Chapter 19

It irked Dan Smith that Corinne had pointedly not been around when he had breakfast and checked out and that put him in a malevolent mood. His bubble filled with the heady gases of superiority and self-assurance had been pricked and he knew it and he didn't like it. So, if that was the little game she wanted to play, then she'd sewn the wind and would assuredly reap the whirlwind, he decided and this made him feel instantly better.

He'd finally run out of steam with his Hidden Gems series after some twenty episodes, so now, if his Features Editor agreed, he'd move on to a new series entitled Ten Years On. This would throw a spotlight on unsuspecting communities a decade after they had been visited by some disaster to see how their wounds had healed. His initial research had thrown up some basic information about the fire at the Old Mill House right there in the very heart of his intended Hidden Gems village and all that had followed, but the reluctance of both Ben Jameson and his sister-in-law Corinne to talk about it had aroused his interest and made him curious. There was already more than enough in the circumstances surrounding the blaze to make Little Oreford the curtain-raiser for his new series. Yes, the more he thought about this, the more he was beginning to relish the thought of teaching Miss Snooty Corinne Potter a lesson she'd probably never forget.

Instead of making straight for the North Devon link road that would have taken him across to join the M5 at Tiverton, he turned off and made for Draymarket and the offices of its local paper, the Draymarket Gazette, which, he knew from a Google search was towards the top of the High Street.

Luckily, he found a parking spot right opposite and wandered into its small front office and asked to speak to the editor. Jackie Benson happened to be out at the time, but a recently appointed junior, overawed by his national paper credentials, said he was sure it would be all right for Dan to come upstairs to the office and search through the large file of bound back copy year books, which was the paper's most valuable resource.

Dan knew he'd hit the jackpot when he casually pulled out the book from the appropriate year, placed it upon the counter and turned to the edition of June 23rd to be confronted with a front- page picture of The Old Mill House taken shortly after a serious fire with Ben Jameson in the foreground over a headline shouting Hero Ben Saves the Day.

"How can I help you?" a voice, not sounding overly friendly, asked from behind him. Dan swung round on his heels to be confronted by a short and stocky woman with dark framed no nonsense glasses who clearly had attitude. "You must be the editor I assume," he said in his most friendly voice while extending a hand which was not immediately taken. "That's right, but I'd be interested to know just what you are doing in my office and going through our files," she replied icily.

At that point and clearly shocked at the stance being taken by his editor, the junior, whose name was Jonathan, hastened to explain that their visitor was Dan Smith from a national newspaper doing some research into a story and he'd invited him up to their office. "Well take a seat Dan," Jackie invited, waving him to a chair at a large and battered wooden desk, strewn with council reports, and opposite hers.

He watched as she pointedly closed the heavy year book, and returned it to its empty slot below the counter. "I feel we've got off slightly on the wrong foot and I do apologise for that," he said, after she'd taken her seat in front of him. "No, Jonathan invited you up so that's OK," she replied. "So, what's your research all about?" Dan hesitated. He was suddenly not sure he should reveal the real reason for wanting to delve into her back copies.

After all this was her domain and it was clear from her initial attitude that she might not take too kindly to what he was proposing, but Jackie Benson gave him no time to gather his thoughts. "I saw you had the book open at our page one lead story on the fire at The Old Mill House in Little Oreford, so what's your interest in that?" It was suddenly clear to Dan the tables had been turned and he was being interviewed and put on the spot, instead of the other way around which was the normal order of things. He was no longer in control and he did not like it. Left with little choice, he explained he'd just come from the village having completed some interviews for his England's Hidden Gems feature series. during which someone had mentioned the serious fire at the mill and that had aroused his curiosity. "The fire was a long time ago now so I hardly see its relevance to a piece extolling the virtues of visiting Little Oreford," she replied.

Jackie sensed immediately there was probably more to this than met the eye and besides that, there was something about this journalist she did not trust. So, if she allowed him further access to their files, he'd quickly learn about the ruthless killings which followed and of that terrible night Ben Jameson smashed a bottle over the head of that psychopathic woman Tanya Thompson.

She'd been in a jealous rage with local estate agent Royston Randall and was probably about to kill him and his future wife, Alicia. No going down that road was certainly not an option. "As I have already explained, the fire was a long time ago and here at The Gazette we like to report on today's happenings and look to the future," she said getting to her feet and signalling that the interview was now over. Dan thanked her for her time and retreated down the stairs feeling humiliated, not an emotion he'd felt for many a year and now more determined than ever to discover the whole story. He'd promised his editor he'd be straight back, but he'd make an excuse and stay on for another day.

He'd noticed a Premier Inn, or was it a Travelodge? on the edge of town, so he'd check in there and do some more digging. He was almost there when he spotted a small fire station, one of the hundreds across the country operated by part time firefighters and there was an appliance being hosed down on the forecourt. That was a bit of luck because they'd probably just returned from a 'shout' otherwise the machine would have been locked behind closed doors. Dan pulled up opposite and wandered over to chat to the fire fighter, which turned out to be much easier than he'd expected because this, obviously older man, glad of an excuse for taking a breather.

After they'd exchanged small talk, Dan asked how long he'd been a retained firefighter in Draymarket and was quietly pleased to hear it had been over twenty years. "Then you probably remember the big blaze at the Old Mill House over at Little Oreford a few years ago," he asked tentatively.

"Certainly do, and all that followed which had the whole community talking about nothing else for weeks. Dan knew he'd hit the jackpot on the first attempt. "So, what did follow?" he asked innocently. "It soon came out that the mill had been used for growing cannabis, right under the noses of the whole village and the two Eastern Europeans, who were running it, were later murdered on a nearby farm!" "Are you all right there, Tom?" a voice which had a note of authority, asked as Dan turned to see what he took probably to be the station officer walking across the forecourt now back in his electrician's overalls. "All nearly finished here, Harry, only this gent was just asking about the famous Little Oreford cannabis farm blaze," he explained. "That was all a long time ago and most people around here have closed the door on all of that and moved on," came the station officer's curt reply. He was immediately thinking of Royston Randall, who was Draymarket Retained Fire Station's main source of charity income for their National Benevolent Fund.

Making a pretence of looking at his watch, Dan said he really should be going and giving them a smile, walked slowly back to his car. This was clearly a town with a story that little people in semi authority didn't want to talk about.

He also knew from his early reporting days that, members of a town's fire, police and ambulance services shared a camaraderie with their local newspaper and that if a stranger suddenly started asking uncomfortable questions, then the word would certainly get about. So, he'd now have to tread more carefully but, unknown to him, it was already too late.

"Hi Jackie, it's Ian here. We've just been to pull a cow out of a ditch at Appletree Farm, a couple of miles out on the Hampton Green Road, which might give you a paragraph or two. Oh! and by the way, we've just had a chap turn up asking questions about the Old Mill House fire which sparked off all that trouble."

Jackie thanked him for the info saying she'd send her new Junior, Jonathan, out to the farm to write a piece because it would be an ideal on-the-job experience for him. So, it looked as if Dan Smith was not going away and just how long would it take him to find his way to Royston's door, she wondered. He and Alicia had a nine-year-old son, who they would almost certainly not have told about that terrible business. Equally importantly, as Royston was chairman of the charitable trust set up to support the Gazette and ensure the town retained its newspaper long after many of those around had ceased publication, she should probably alert him as to what had just happened. But then she had second thoughts because the news coming right out of the blue was bound to worry him and Alicia, probably unnecessarily, so she'd just keep an eye on the situation, she decided.

Chapter 20

Bob's thoughts were in turmoil as he drove slowly back to Hampton Green. He was in love with Annie, but not at all sure he'd ever want to swap his life beside the sea and the roving business he'd built up there, for the small towns and mostly narrow roads and lanes of this particular part of North Devon.
Still the chances were that Miss Charlotte would not find a suitable property, almost certainly not in a single day, and by the time one did come along, she'd probably have gone off the whole idea anyway, he told himself. Both Hannah and Heather were out when he got back to the barn, which pleased him because he could stroll over to the Red Lion for a pint and some supper and enjoy a bit of quality time to himself, but they pounced on his return and without thinking, he told them of the old lady's latest plan. "Little Oreford Court!" they said as one and almost without hesitation. "It could be perfect because it's almost half way between Little Oreford and Yardley Upton and has been on the market for ages," said Hannah. "So, what's wrong with it?" asked Bob, beginning to have a horrible feeling that things weren't going quite as he'd hoped. "There's nothing wrong with it other than it's too large for a family house, over-priced

and in a slightly out of the way place," explained Heather. "We have the details and the keys in the office and I could come up and show Mrs Andrews around tomorrow morning," she offered. It was now just after 10pm so was that too late to call Annie again? He'd had a long chat with her while having supper and discovered she too had very mixed feelings about Charlie's suggestion.

No, he would give her a quick call about the property and that Charlie could view it in the morning, which he knew she'd want to the moment she was told about it. Annie had been on the phone to her bosses at Ocean View who were not at all keen on their star guest spending another week away and needed their Duty Manager back because they were short staffed the following week. Sam Owen wasn't in a good mood. He didn't like it when arrangements did not go according to his plan and all of a sudden. Annie wasn't at all sure she wanted to go back to Ocean View and work for them anymore. She'd already checked and Corinne had confirmed that Charlie could keep her room and there'd be room for her too. She could hear Sally Owen saying in the background that if Miss Charlotte wanted to stay on then there was little they could do about it, but that their Duty Manager must return with Bob.

Unknown to all, Charlie had just spent almost an hour on a call to her stepson James in the Caribbean. She'd been his 'Ma' since the age of seven and, mirroring her own childhood freedom, she'd allowed him almost a completely free reign around the complex where they lived and the nearby beach where he'd already learned to sail and snorkel. They were both free spirits and quickly developed a close bond. In the early days, Charlie had kept some independence by continuing to work for the large hotel and leisure complex she'd originally flown out to help open, but as soon as they were married, she switched to helping her husband Hugo with his ever-expanding business, developing apartment resorts right across the Caribbean.

He was already a wealthy man before they met, but by the time of his sudden death from a massive heart attack in his 67th year the family were 'loaded.' By this time, James Andrews was heavily involved in the business and easily assumed his father's mantle, but after her beloved Hugo's death, Charlie's heart slowly went out of it and then her stepson met and married a woman, with whom, try as she might, she could not get on. Charlie had kept in close touch with Jean, a hotel General Manager colleague, who'd recently retired to a Victorian villa on the hillside overlooking Sidmouth and knowing of her friend's growing unhappiness with her situation, she invited Charlie to visit for a long holiday with a view to it becoming a permanent arrangement if it suited. It had suited and once settled in Devon, Charlie came to the conclusion that she would not go back to the Caribbean, except to escape to the sun between mid-January and the end of March. This she and Jean did for the eight happy years they lived as companions.

Her relationship with her daughter-in-law mellowed as time passed and the two almost started to like one another. But all came to a sudden end with Jean's death from a particularly aggressive cancer and that was when Charlie went to live at Ocean View.

"James, I've returned for a holiday to Little Oreford, the small North Devon village where I grew up and now feel that I want to leave Ocean View and come and live here as soon as I've found a suitable house, large enough for a housekeeper and someone to drive me around." There was a pause.

It was mid-afternoon in the Caribbean and James had only been half listening to Charlie because he was right in the middle of a business transaction, but now he was on full alert! "Ma. Do you really want to have all that upheaval at your time of life? The last time I came to see you at Ocean View you told me how nice the place was and that it suited you very well," he pointed out. "That was then Jimmy and this is now and I'm really looking forward to having a new adventure and besides I already have two young friends in mind to come and live with me." Her stepson knew from long experience there was absolutely no chance of persuading his stepmother to do other than what she wanted, once she'd made her mind up about something. She was certainly a chip off the old block or would have been if she'd actually been his Ma. "Look, Ma, if this is what you really want, then that's absolutely fine by me so let me know when you've found a place that suits and I'll come over or send someone suitable to do the business."

Annie spent a restless night, knowing she wanted to be with Bob, who'd clearly be reluctant to leave Sidmouth, but not wanting to be sucked back into her previous life at Ocean View. So, the surprising fact that Heather and Hannah had actually come up with a suitable property for Charlie and that they'd all be viewing it later that morning had thrown her into a complete turmoil.

As she had known full well, Charlie was more than excited on hearing Bob's news about Little Oreford Court the following morning, and that Heather would be arriving with the keys around 11am.

"Even the name sounds right," she declared as they followed Heather out of Little Oreford and along the lane towards Yardley Upton for a couple of miles before turning off into a well-maintained gravel drive.
Charlie knew at first sight she'd found her future home. Little Oreford Court was a substantial three-storey stone-built property with a large, but later added granny annexe on one side and at right angles to an original two storey stable block clearly ripe for conversion for residential use. Heather, led the way, entering the covered entrance porch and unlocking the oak front door, explaining as she did so that the property had been empty since the previous autumn despite a number of viewings and was now classed by Royston Randall as one of his 'stickers' properties. "Believe it or not, Albany House was also branded 'a sticker' before the Jameson's moved in," she recalled. Stepping through the large oak-floored entrance hall into a substantial and expensively-carpeted lounge, Charlie declared that Little Oreford Court was not going to be a 'sticker' any longer. "I'm going to need a lot of furniture and you and Hannah are going to have to help me with that," she said turning to Heather. Then she was remembering all that her unsuspecting daughter Laura had told her about the exciting time she and Margo had had furnishing Albany

House. It was almost as if a decade later, history was going to be repeating itself and it gave her a warm and excited feeling.

Once back at the inn, she made another call to her stepson confirming that, believe it or not, she'd actually found the house where she wished to remain for the rest of her days.

Then she put James on to Corinne, who assured him that his mother was now being treated as one of the family and that they'd do anything necessary to help her secure her dream.

"The first thing Ma's going to need is a good local lawyer to handle the conveyancing and I am assuming you can recommend someone," he said to Corinne, immediately getting down to business.

Annie drove back to Sidmouth with Bob on the Saturday morning having also been assured by Corinne that she and her sister Laura would keep a close eye on Mrs Andrews and treat her as one of their own. Not long after they'd driven away, Heather returned to Little Oreford and drove Charlie, not back to Royston Randall's original Hampton Green office, but to their Head Office in the Draymarket High Street where, tipped off by Hannah, Royston had driven in, especially to meet her. Also standing at the reception desk, immaculately suited and booted with an expensive brown leather briefcase in hand was leading local solicitor Henry Robinson who'd been called by Corinne and then instructed in a call from the Caribbean. As soon as the initial paperwork had been completed for a sale at the asking price of £840,000, the funds for the deposit would be transferred, it had been agreed.

Chapter 21

Being single, but married to her profession, Jackie Benson was also in her office further up the High that Saturday morning and happened to pop out to do a bit of shopping. She spotted Royston in his front office, highly unusual for a weekend, so it was the perfect opportunity to pop in and explain what had been on her mind since Thursday morning when Dan Smith had suddenly turned up. Closeted together in his boardroom, she told him the little she knew about Dan Smith, together with a few particulars she'd gleaned from the 'net.' "He's a bona fide national journalist all right but the fact that he started asking questions at the fire station after I thought I'd probably headed him off, makes me slightly worried. Seeing he'd already been to Little Oreford to research for his Hidden Gems travel series, I called Corinne Potter at the Oreford Inn and she confirmed he'd stayed with them on the Wednesday night, but also said that she'd not particularly taken to him. To tell you the truth I don't think there's a lot more we can do other than wait to see what appears in his Hidden Gems piece." Royston agreed, saying they should keep this to themselves because, he saw no point in worrying Alicia at the moment.

Dan parked up and checked in to the Travel Lodge before walking back into town later on that previous Thursday morning. Entering The Carpenter's Arms, he pulled up a stool beside the bar, ordered a pint and casually engaged the barman in conversation, which he continued between customers. He later ordered a snack and remained at the bar surreptitiously turning his attention to those he figured out to be regulars.

By mid-afternoon he'd worked his way slowly through four or five pints and had, he believed, harvested the essence of the story that had so shocked this quiet community a decade earlier and would make a sensational curtain raiser for his new series. The question was whether he should call on Royston and Alicia Randall and ask them about the night that psychopathic woman stalker gatecrashed his home and was about to shoot them both when Ben Jameson had rushed in and smashed her over the head with a bottle. He would, of course, also have to go back to Little Oreford and re interview Ben who'd be sure to tell his sister-in-law Corinne, he thought with a smug satisfaction. But no there was another less confrontational way. He'd go back to the hotel, which had an eatery attached to it, have a quiet night, write up his notes and drive back to Oxford early the following morning. Then when he'd chased up on official police and court records via some Freedom of Information requests and teased out as many other elements of the story as possible, he would write the piece up and send it to Ben Jameson and to Royston and Alicia Randall by recorded delivery seeking their comments prior to publication.

At Charlie's meeting with Royston in his office that Saturday morning, the newly appointed solicitor said if all went according to plan, exchange of contracts and completion of the property sale could go through in around four weeks, or be timed to coincide with Mrs Andrews' planned return to the village. Later, Heather took Charlie out for coffee and a wander around the still thriving High Street before they were joined by Hannah for a light lunch.

It didn't take Charlie, now in her most gregarious element, long to persuade the pair to take her back to Little Oreford Court for another good look around and to begin planning how she should furnish her three reception rooms, large kitchen, five ensuite bedrooms, family bathrooms on both floors and large south-facing Victorian-style conservatory. Both Hannah and Heather were now fully committed to helping Charlie furnish her new home so they spent most of that afternoon going from room making some initial notes on how each should be furnished, before finally dropping her back at The Oreford a little after 5pm.

The sun was still blazing down on the green, casting black shadows on the edge of the grass from the row of beeches leading their shady way along the church drive. "I'll go and sit in the churchyard for a while because I've got so much to think about," she said to herself. Luckily there was no one occupying her shady seat as there had been the other morning so, on an impulse, she reached into a pocket to make sure the business card one of those nice journalists had given her was still there. Charlie was deep in thought when something made her look up to see Lottie coming out of the church and walking down the path towards her but she could she immediately that her granddaughter was upset. "Oh, I'm so glad it's you," said Lottie sitting down beside her while fighting to keep back her tears. Charlie reached out, instinctively taking her by the hand. "What is it Lottie? Why are you so upset? Have you and Andy split up by any chance?" she asked with concern in her voice. "Oh no it's the very opposite from that," said her granddaughter, suddenly burying her head in Charlie's shoulder and beginning to weep.

"I went into the chemist in Draymarket for a pregnancy test kit this morning and it's come out positive for the second week running!" she revealed. "Oh dear. Have you told Andy yet?" she asked. "No, we went to the coast the other day and I meant to do it then, but somehow I just couldn't bring myself to because I was hoping against hope that when I took the second test it would be negative, but it wasn't and now I've wrecked our lives because the minute I tell mum and dad, Andy will be asked to leave and I might never see him again," she said, tears now flowing uncontrollably. They sat in silence for a few minutes until her granddaughter's sobs had subsided. "No, dear, I'm absolutely positive that's the last thing that's going to happen once they've calmed down and realised just how much in love you both are." said Charlie giving her granddaughter's hand a gentle squeeze and instantly remembering that momentous afternoon all those years ago when she'd stormed out of Albany House, three months pregnant and vowing never to return. Oh, how very different was this situation, if only her granddaughter knew. "Now listen dear, you must, of course, tell Andy as soon as you have some time together, but don't tell your parents yet because I have a plan," she confided. "What sort of plan?" Lottie asked between her tears, but now feeling a small sense of relief that she'd shared her terrible secret. "After you've had the baby, you and Andy are going to need somewhere to live close by and luckily, I can now help with that." "But how?" asked Lottie, producing a small packet of tissues from her bag and wiping away her tears. "Well, I'm about to buy Little Oreford Court, so that I can come and live hereabouts.

"I went to see it for the first time yesterday and it has a large granny annex, which would be ideal for you and Andy and the baby," she revealed. "Oh, Mrs Andrews, could we really come and live with you?" asked Lottie, beginning for the first time to see a small chink of light and a ray of hope for the future. "Of, course you can, so now you have something positive to tell Andy. But listen dear, please, please, don't tell your parents yet, because I can see a way of making it easier for them to accept your news and you would want that wouldn't you?"

The two walked slowly back towards the inn and Albany House, arm in comforting arm and as they did so, a taxi pulled up outside the thatched cottage on the far side of the green and an elderly couple got out. "Oh, Uncle Robin and Auntie Margo are back from their cruise, but I don't think I want to go over and welcome them home in this state. because they'll be sure to see I've been crying," she resolved. "So, you have an uncle and aunt living in the village as well," replied Charlie feigning her surprise. "No, they sort of adopted Luke and me when we were kids because they are brother and sister and have none of their own, and I'd say they're mum and dad's closest friends," she said. "That's really nice, Lottie," replied Charlie, wondering if her childhood friends had never married or had had partners, who had either died or been divorced, but she'd find out soon enough. They parted outside the inn with Lottie again promising not to break the news to her parents for the time being.

Corinne just happened to be standing in the inn doorway and saw from their body language just how close her niece and their enigmatic guest seemed to have become. "Welcome back Mrs Andrews.

"I think you must have had quite an exciting day and I can't tell you just how delighted Laura, Ben and I are that you are going to become part of our little community." Charlie said she was delighted too. "But I think it's time you stopped calling me Mrs Andrews, when Charlie will do, because I never did like my proper name, which is Charlotte," she replied, noting that Corinne had wasted little time telling her sister and Ben the news. "As you so rightly say, it has been an exciting day, but also quite a tiring one so if I could have a pot of tea in the lounge and a light supper, perhaps some smoked salmon sandwiches, sent up to my room then that would be lovely."

Sitting in her armchair overlooking the green at dusk, she saw the lights come on in Robin and Margo's cottage and tried to imagine what would happen when she walked over and knocked on their door later the following morning. And what would they say when they learned that their adopted grandchildren were hers!

Chapter 22

It had been a long and tiring journey home after Robin and Margo Lloyd had disembarked from Fred Olsen's classic cruise ship MV Boudicca in Liverpool and they'd stayed up later than intended doing all their unpacking, so it was around 11am when Robin eventually emerged from his room and wandered downstairs to make a cuppa. Normally Margo was always up before him, but he could hear she was still fast asleep as he'd tiptoed past her bedroom door. Still in his dressing gown, he took his cuppa out through the conservatory to their old bench on the patio and sat awhile admiring their garden now in full bloom, when the doorbell rang. "Blast that'll wake Margs," he muttered, hurrying through the house and opening the front door before it rang again to be faced by a smartly-dressed woman of about his own age.

"I'm so sorry. I've called too early. Look I'll come back again after lunch," said Charlie, taking a step backwards. "Who is it Robin?" Margo called from behind him now half way down the stairs, having already dressed. Charlie stood there hesitantly, now not knowing quite what to do because things weren't working out quite as she imagined they might. Then Margo was beside Robin in the doorway. "Don't worry we're never normally up this late, so how can we help?" she asked. "This is going to sound awfully rude, but I'm staying over at the inn for a few days and the manager happened to mention that you had an amazing cottage garden and I wondered if I might have a look around it because I so love gardens," she explained.

"We'd be delighted to show you," she said, stepping aside to let their surprise visitor enter. "Are you sure because I can easily call back after lunch. "Yes of course we're sure aren't we Robin?"

A few minutes later Charlie was sitting in their lounge, a room she'd been in so many times before and looking about her while Margo made coffee and Robin had gone up to dress. All was still very much as it had been in her day with the large stone fireplace and exposed stone chimney breast and 'goodness me,' there was the original copper coal scuttle with its tongs and long-handled fork. "I thought we'd have coffee indoors rather than walking around outside with mugs, said Margo, coming in with a tray and sitting down opposite her and now being joined by Robin. Charlie took a deep Breath. I think it's probably time to introduce myself properly and to tell you what brings me to Little Oreford," she announced, her heart beginning to race. "I am known hereabouts as Mrs Charlotte Andrews, presently residing at The Ocean View retirement hotel in Sidmouth, but you will remember me far better as Charlie Potter, the errant younger daughter of the Rev Will Potter, late of this parish and your childhood friend." She studied the sheer look of amazement on her friends' faces. "Is it really you, Charlie?" gasped Margo, putting her hands to her face. "Good Lord, I can see that it is now!" uttered Robin, getting to his feet and coming over to give Charlie a bear hug as she too rose to her feet with Margo joining in. Once they were all seated again with the coffee going cold in their mugs, Charlie warned them to prepare themselves for yet another shock.

"I'm not sure I can cope with another one and it certainly couldn't be as surprising as the last one," said Robin. "I wouldn't be quite so sure," replied Charlie. now beginning to enjoy keeping her oldest friends in such suspense. "Come on. You can't keep us on tenterhooks any longer," joined in Margo. Charlie took another deep breath. "Firstly, it was certainly a surprise and a delight to learn from Lottie that you had become her much-loved uncle and aunt when she and Luke were youngsters and that Laura and Ben think of you as their closest friends," she explained. "My, you are well-informed," said Robin, wondering just what on earth was coming next. Charlie had told them she'd only been staying at the inn for a week, yet she already seemed to have made friends with the Jameson family and was on first name terms with them. "Come on Charlie, out with it," said Margo, equally mystified over her obvious friendship with their friends. It was suddenly as if they were all kids again and they were urging her to reveal the latest adventurous scheme she'd cooked up. "To tell you the truth, when I decided to pay a return visit after all these years, I did wonder where you might be now but I never expected you'd still be here and in the same house," admitted Charlie. "Well, we haven't been here all the time, but we did come back after our parents had both died," explained Margo. "While it was a great surprise to discover you were still here, that was nothing compared to the shock I got when on checking in, I spotted the name Corinne Potter on the manager's badge!" "Good Lord," uttered Robin again, immediately realising the connection.

"Yes, Corinne is one of my babies, who was taken into care in Bristol when she was six months old!" revealed Charlie. "And just imagine how I felt when I learned that her sister, Laura, who I gave up at birth, had also somehow found her way back here, and later saw that they were identical twins!" she continued quietly. "This is truly all quite unbelievable Charlie," said Margo shaking her head. "But do your girls know?"

There was a pause. "No because I've been trying to work out just when and how I should break the news. I had thought at first, I might tiptoe quietly away knowing that all was well in their world, because just how might they react to a mother who'd abandoned them?" She suddenly felt close to tears. "Charlie, we know you'd never have done such a thing unless you were desperate and there was no other way," said Margo.

A hastily-assembled lunch was prepared because there was no way they were going to allow Charlie to go back to the inn before they'd heard her life story right from the day she'd left Little Oreford. They ate at a table on the patio with Charlie now wanting to know what had become of her family and especially her sister, Cynthia.

"As we've told you, we were both busy pursuing our separate careers in London, but we did keep up with the local news on visits home to see mum and dad, said Margo.

"Cynthia never did leave home and sadly died from breast cancer in her mid-forties. Your father soldiered on as rector until his death and your mother lived on for another ten years or so with the house falling into disrepair all around her.

It was eventually left to a nephew and remained on the market for quite a time until Robin and I stepped in and bought it as an investment and to rent to Laura and Ben."

Wandering around the garden with Robin later, Charlie turned a corner and was amazed to come across a perfect model village replica of Little Oreford, now a little worse for wear from the weather and neglect. "I made it some years ago and your grandchildren used to love helping me with it, but I really should demolish it now, although I can't bring myself to do it at the moment," he said. They re-joined Margo on the patio. "Just how are you going to break your news," she pressed. "Well, what if I arrange a small dinner party, say on Thursday evening, and hopefully find an opportune moment to tell them then?" she suggested. But oh dear, I don't think the inn has a private dining room," she added. "No, they don't," Robin agreed. "But we can host it here, can't we Margs? Our conservatory is plenty big enough," he pointed out. "Of course, we can, so that's settled then," she declared. "That would be wonderful and really special seeing they also have no idea we're childhood friends. But there's only one condition and that is that we ask Corinne and her catering team to provide the food and bring it over," she insisted. That sounds just perfect so we can devote our time to simply playing hosts," agreed Margo, who, considered herself a little past throwing a dinner party for so many guests.

Corinne Potter, under renewed instructions from Annie to keep a special eye out for Mrs Andrews seeing that she and Bob would not be around after Saturday, happened to spot her walking across the green that morning and disappearing into Margo and Robin's. She was more than a little surprised when she did not return to the inn till gone 4.30pm. It amused her when she remembered that Mrs Andrews had described the obviously well-meaning pair as her 'Minders. Yes, there was an awful lot more to their VIP guest than first met the eye, which was immediately confirmed when Charlie wondered if she might spare a few moments to pop into the lounge for a chat. "I would like to throw a small dinner party on Thursday evening as a 'thank you' to you all for making me feel so welcome and almost like one of the family since my arrival. The Lloyds, whom I met this morning, have generously offered to play hosts, which I accepted on the understanding that, hopefully, you would be able to provide the food at my expense, of course, and just bring it over," she explained "I'm sure we can handle that, but might I suggest we prepare a hot and cold help yourself buffet together with some sweets and a cheese board?" she suggested. "That sounds a simply excellent idea. I'm feeling excited about it already," said Charlie. "I do hope that you and Laura and Ben and Lottie and Luke will be able to come along, plus Hannah and Heather, who are going to be helping me furnish Little Oreford Court, and also one other young man who has yet to confirm." Charlie said she'd go up to her room for a rest before coming down to supper and might she call Laura and Ben to see if they and the children would be free which she really hoped they would.

"Oh! and one other thing; could she tell Laura that she'd like to have another little chat with Lottie if she could pop in for a couple of minutes either tomorrow or Tuesday."

"Honestly Laura I'm beginning to have this really bizarre feeling that Mrs Andrews, whose suddenly come into our lives, is working some charm spell that's got us all dancing around after her," said Corinne on the phone to her sister five minutes later. "She's only known Robin and Margo five minutes and now they're hosting this dinner party for her. And she also seems to have developed quite a friendship with Lottie," she remarked. "That's probably a good thing because she's seemed a little distracted of late," admitted Laura. "She says she's

OK but I'm sure there's something on her mind that she's not telling us about."

Heather had a day off on Monday, so she again picked up Charlie around 10am and they went over to Little Oreford Court to measure up for curtains before driving on to a fabrics and soft furnishing store in the Allway Centre. But they had to be back by 2:30pm to meet up with an architect, who had been recommended to them, to come up with some suggestions for converting the old stables into a garage with accommodation above.

Chapter 23

Commis Chef Andy was on a day off and had arranged to meet Lottie after college. He'd parked in his usual spot on a side road and they were soon ensconced in a quiet corner of one of the Allway Centre's fast-food outlets. It was here she broke the news that she was now around ten weeks pregnant! She'd burst into tears when sharing her news with Charlie, but now she was being strong for both of them. "How long have you known?" he asked, taking both her hands in his and telling her he loved her very much. "Don't worry we'll have our baby together and I'll figure out a way we can manage afterwards," he assured her. "Oh! Andy, will you? I was so afraid you would not want me once you found out," she admitted, now with tears in her eyes. "Not want you, now I want you more than ever," he replied. They sat quietly holding hands for a few moments and then Lottie broke the silence. "It's going to be awful telling my parents, especially as we've kept our relationship from them because they'll say we've been deceitful and that'll probably hurt them just as much as me being pregnant," she said. "I know but with me being a vegetable chopper in the kitchen, and you being the boss's niece, it did seem best not to say anything at the time," he pointed out. "Yes, we can explain that to them in which case they might not feel so hurt," said Lottie. "So, when are we going to tell your parents then? It's not going to be so bad for me because mine hardly speak to me anyway," he pointed out. Lottie took a deep breath.

"We could go home and do it straight away, but Mrs Andrews, this amazing guest who came to stay a week ago and arrived in a Bentley with a chauffeur and companion, wants us to wait until the end of the week. "She's buying Little Oreford Court, just down the road, and says we can go and live in her granny annex together after the baby's born." A silence fell between them with Andy feeling an immediate sting of hurt that Lottie had actually broken her news to this stranger before telling him, but kept it too himself. "Why put if off for a week and how's that going to help anyway?" he asked. "Because Mrs Andrews is having a dinner party at Auntie Margo's and Uncle Robin's on Thursday night and wants us both to go. Sort of like coming out into the open about our relationship," she explained. "What! me, coming out of the kitchen and suddenly turning up at a posh dinner party with your close family. No way! She must be mad to have even made such a weird suggestion!" he protested. "Look Andy, it's not going to be so bad because when I get home, I'm going to tell my parents and Auntie Corinne about us, but not about the baby, and explain why we kept it a secret and tell them we wished we hadn't and I know they'll understand. Luckily, you're not working this week, so you won't be in the kitchen tomorrow and all you'll have to do is to turn up on Thursday and we'll both go over to Auntie Margo's and Uncle Robins together." Andy began shaking his head."I'm really not sure I can do this because we won't be getting everything over in one go. One minute they find out we're together and then five minutes later we announce we're expecting a baby!" he pointed out. "Look Andy. I've been going over and over again in my head with all this since I told Mrs Andrews and I really, really, think it's the best thing to do."

A single tear trickled down her cheek which was more than enough to overwhelm all his misgivings.

"I just knew there was something troubling Lottie and now we know what it was all about," said Laura as she and Ben climbed into bed. "Corinne says Andy's a really nice lad, conscientious and hard-working and gets on well with everybody so I really wished she'd told us ages ago, especially as they've been keeping this a secret all these months," she said. "Yes, but I can still see it from their point of view. Once you go down the road of being secretive about something, then the longer it goes on the more difficult it is to come out with it," said Ben. "So, what have you been keeping secret from me?" said Laura suddenly drawing close to him and feeling a tingling urge welling up inside her. She'd just known there was something troubling their daughter for weeks and now it was all out in the open, it was as if her relief had suddenly stirred up other emotions. "I was thinking about those times when I was so unhappy under all the pressures of being a hospital administrator, but somehow couldn't bring myself to tell you," he recalled. "Well, we can forget all about that now, Mr Ben," she said beginning to pull down his pyjama bottoms!

Thursday did not get off to a good start for Corinne. She had a dozen members of the Draymarket Rotary Club in for lunch, six other table reservations, and a full complement of hotel guests, plus all the food to prepare for tonight's dinner party. She would have managed, but her morning waitress had called in sick and so had John, a member of the kitchen team, so it was all hands to the pump.

She knew Lottie and Luke were at home so a quick call and they were both over to help out with serving the breakfasts, but an extra pair of hands were definitely going to be needed in the kitchen. "Don't worry Auntie Corinne. Call Andy and I know he'll come in and help out." The relief of just being able to make that suggestion gave Lottie such a thrill she forgot for an instant that she was also pregnant. He was still asleep when his mobile woke him, having spent most of the night agonising over the prospect of the dinner party and then having to break the news to Lottie's parents that she was pregnant. "Andy, is that you?" Corinne asked, having never called her young Commis Chef on his mobile before. The unmistakeable sound of his boss's voice hit him like a bucket of ice-cold water and he was instantly awake and fearing retribution. "Yes, Miss Potter," he replied hesitantly. "Oh good. Look I know you're on holiday, but John's called in sick and we're very short staffed in the kitchen and we've a busy day ahead so can you come in?" she asked. "Of course. I'll be straight over," he replied feeling instantly relieved this had not been about him and Lottie and would be a chance to improve his standing before they broke the news. There was a pause. "Look Andy, you really should have told us all about you and Lottie and I think we need to talk about that later, but it's enough is to say that we're all fine about it, albeit a little disappointed that you both chose to keep your relationship secret rather than sharing it with us," she said. "We know it was mistake, but it just sort-of worked out that way," he replied. "OK that's all for now and don't race over because I need you here in one piece."

Andy did race over because there wasn't a moment to lose in making it up to the family and he now had the faint hope that when they did break the news of Lottie's pregnancy, it might not be that bad after all. Even the boss telling him she needed him there 'in one piece' made him feel that perhaps there was more to the comment than her requirement for another pair of hands in the kitchen. Despite his haste, he'd also remembered to throw his best casuals into a bag in preparation for the party while still hoping there might be a convenient way of avoiding it, perhaps by having to work on in the kitchen which would be the perfect excuse.

Chapter 24

Charlie had also spent a disturbed night going over and over in her head how to break her momentous news at her party and was lying awake when there came a tentative knock on her bedroom door. She knew instantly this wasn't the normal knock announcing the arrival of her breakfast or supper, but she still called out and invited her visitor in. "Oh! it's you, Lottie. Come in dear and close the door and come and sit on the edge of the bed, she invited. "Luke and I have been helping out with the breakfasts, but the rush is over so I thought I'd pop up and tell you that I told Mum and Dad about me and Andy last night and they were really cool about it. Auntie Corinne, who also knows, asked him to come in and help out this morning because they're one down in the kitchen so I'm feeling a whole lot better about everything, although I'm still dreading what they'll say when they hear our real news," she admitted. "Never meet trouble half way dear. That's the good advice I was given when I was not much older than you, by a dear friend, who was also called Corinne, like your aunt. So, have you also told everyone you're bringing Andy to my little party tonight?" Lottie said she had and that he'd reluctantly agreed to come. When her unsuspecting granddaughter had gone downstairs, Charlie got up, dressed and went down to the dining room where Corinne showed her the dinner menu she'd just prepared and printed off. "That's wonderful, Corinne dear. I do appreciate all you and your family have done to make me feel so welcome here and I can't wait to really become part of your community when I move into Little Oreford Court."

It had been arranged that everyone would arrive at Robin and Margo's around 7pm by which time all the dishes would have been delivered and laid out in the kitchen and on a trestle table, which Ben had carried over from mill. It was a little after 6pm when Charlie arrived and accepted a large gin and tonic from Robin, who took her through to the conservatory where Margo had just finished laying the table. "It's going to be a bit of a squeeze with nine, but I'm sure it will all be fine," she said coming over and giving Charlie a hug. "Lottie's just popped in and told us about Andy, which was a bit of a surprise because we never realized she had a young man, although we sort of recognised him. But talking of introductions, have you had any further thoughts on how you might begin breaking your news tonight?" Margo asked. "I've thought about little else over the past twenty-four hours and it's occurred to me that perhaps after Robin, has said a few words of welcome, I could reveal I'm the daughter of the former Rev Will Potter and that you are my childhood friends. "Charlie that's inspirational because the girls will immediately spot the connection and start putting two and two together, which will sort of soften the blow" she pointed out. "Well let's wait and see. I'm feeling pretty nervous about it all, to tell you the truth, and, who knows, I might not have the strength to actually go through with it even now," she admitted. "Don't worry because we're with you whatever you decide to do," said Margo. Just then the doorbell rang announcing arrival of the hot food, which they all hurriedly carried in and arranged on a series of Chinese restaurant-style hot plates on the large farmhouse kitchen table.

Minutes later, Hannah and Heather arrived and quickly monopolised Charlie, taking her mind off all that was to follow.

Before she knew it, Laura and Ben had come in, followed by Luke and Lottie and then by Corinne, who'd made a point of rescuing Andy from the kitchen and suggesting he got changed in the office because all the guest rooms were taken and there was a party in the residents' lounge. "Thanks for being so understanding, Miss Potter," he said as they walked across the green together. "No, thank you for giving up your time today and I think it's time you dropped the Miss Potter and switched to Corinne, don't you?" Andy was no sooner through the door looking uncertain and feeling way out of his depth when Lottie came over and, taking him by the hand, led him into the kitchen to introduce him to Robin and Margo and then through into the conservatory to meet Laura and Ben. "Mum and Dad, this is Andy." She looked so radiant, both their hearts melted in an instant. Corinne joined them and told how Andy, who'd help save the day in the kitchen, had become really good at filleting fresh fish and had also turned his hand to carving vegetable sculptures for table centre pieces on special occasions. "Perhaps you should pop into the Old Mill in your spare time and also try your hand at woodcarving," invited Ben. Andy said he'd like that and the two continued the conversation as they all wandered back into the lounge, summoned by a call from Margo. "Now everyone it's time to sit down, but first you must all fill your plates from the splendid buffet prepared by Corinne and her team and generously provided by Mrs Charlie Andrews."

Hannah and Heather, having already consumed almost a bottle of chilled white wine between them, were already in party mode when everyone returned to the table and were in the midst of discussing the forthcoming stable block conversion at Little Oreford Court with Charlie. Luke, not been best pleased at having to give up a surfing trip to help out at the inn, was deep in conversation with Andy, who was saying he'd like to get into the sport and that maybe Luke could teach him. Lottie, now sitting between them was feeling ignored and left out as they talked across her. Yes, she was pleased and relieved at just how easily Andy had been accepted into her family, but she wasn't so happy that his attention was now being completely monopolised by her older brother. He'd always been the one at the centre of all the attention while they were growing up and now, here he was doing it again! That wasn't quite true, but he'd always been far more demanding while she was the easy-going little sister.

Corinne and Margo were the last to come to the table after supervising the serving of the buffet, and took their places opposite Laura, Ben and Robin, where a conversation began about journalist Dan Smith. "While you two were sunning yourselves on your cruise, we had a visit from this national paper journalist. He'd come here to throw a spotlight on us for his Hidden English Gems weekend magazine series so hopefully it will generate some more visitors for the mill, although we didn't really take to him, did we, Corinne?" said Ben. Charlie was only half listening to Hannah and Heather, seated on either side of her, as she looked around the table to see everyone chatting happily away to one another.

That was everyone except Lottie, who she could see, was caught in a crossfire of conversation, between Andy and her grandson and not looking very happy about it. Robin seemed to have forgotten all about doing his crucial welcome speech, so perhaps there might come an opportune moment later in the evening to tell them all the truth.

Lottie, now in a highly emotional state, having been completely excluded from the boys' conversation, with several of her attempted interventions waved aside, had finally had enough. "Of, course there won't be much time for surfing once our baby comes!" she said raising her voice in order to be heard. Every now and again, when a group of family or friends are talking together, there will come a moment of silence and it was into that void that Lottie's comment so neatly fell.

All heads turned. She had their full attention. "Yes. I'm ten weeks pregnant. We'd planned to break the news later, hadn't we Andy, but now with us all gathered together it suddenly seemed the right moment," she said, reaching across and taking his hand defiantly in hers. There followed a stony silence, filled with looks of shock and disbelief, but before anyone had any further time to gather their thoughts, Charlie was on her feet in an instant.

"Yes. They're both very much in love and they'll be coming to live in my annex at Little Oreford Court when the baby comes, but before any of you leap to judgement, I have an announcement of my own to make." All heads turned so fading the spotlight on Lottie and Andy.

"I was booked in to your wonderful Oreford Inn, where everyone has made me so very welcome, as Mrs Charlotte Andrews presently residing at The Ocean View Retirement Hotel in Sidmouth. But I am no stranger to this place because I grew up here with Robin and Margo being my childhood friends." Now all heads instantly turned to their hosts, who simply nodded in acceptance, but made no attempt to speak as they turned their attention back to Charlie who was beginning to fight back her tears.

My name is Charlie Potter, the errant older daughter of the Rev and Mrs Will Potter, late of Albany House, who walked out of their lives forever being three months pregnant and out of wedlock with twin daughters whom I named Laura and Corinne. Yes, I was a desperate single mum with no money and no prospects so I gave you both up and have spent my whole lifetime regretting it. So please, please, feel only joy for Lottie, who has grown up loved and wanted, and for her Andy, whom you all know to be a hard- working and decent young man!"

"Oh my God," cried Laura throwing her hands up to her face and bursting into tears. Corinne tried for a few moments to keep her emotions under control, but it was useless. Laura was already on her feet and in a moment they both wrapped their arms around Charlie and wept.

The Epilogue

Charlie never did return to Ocean View, staying on in her room at the Oreford Inn with the whole family now helping to furnish and equip Little Oreford Court and to help Lottie and Andy prepare a room in the annex for the baby. It only took Annie a couple of days back in her old routine at Ocean View to realise she'd had enough both of the place and of her always penny-pinching employers and handed in her notice. While she took no persuading to move in with Bob, she found herself really missing Charlie, who'd started calling her with progress reports on the conversion of the old stable block and with all too obvious hints that it would be just perfect for them. Bob was quickly back into his comfortable routine, but happily agreed they should book in with Heather and Hannah and return to Little Oreford for a long, catch up with everyone, weekend, which was to include another evening at Royston and Alicia's.

Royston, briefed by his Girl Fridays, knew all about Charlie's desire to have the couple come and live with her at Little Oreford Court and that had given him an idea. He was becoming tired of driving all over Devon and into Cornwall visiting his ever- expanding network of branches, so why not employ a chauffeur, who could do all the driving while he worked? He broached the idea while he and Bob were looking at his classic car collection and made him an offer he simply couldn't refuse.

All seemed to be falling neatly into place, until the morning some three months later when two large recorded delivery envelopes were delivered simultaneously to Ben and Corinne.

Inside was Dan Smith's now thoroughly-researched 'Ten Years On' feature describing in great detail all that had happened following the fire at the Old Mill and asking them for their comments. He'd abandoned his last intended Hidden Gems piece and persuaded his editor that the earlier happenings at Little Oreford would make a great curtain-raiser for his new series.

When Charlie was told about it, she suddenly remembered the card given to her by that journalist and his colleague she'd chanced to meet in the churchyard that sunny morning, so she called him to see if he might be able to offer her worried family some advice. By one of those many millions to one chances people have simply given up trying to fathom, he happened to be Dan Smith's Editor. So, after a lengthy conversation in which she explained all the needless hurt that would be caused if he published 'Little Oreford Ten Years On,' she promised that if he could possibly see his way clear to ditching it, then she had a far better story to tell.

THE END

NEXT: Read Albany House – Part Three:
What Happened in Costa Rica

Printed in Great Britain
by Amazon